SOMEONE IS OUT THERE

CAROLE STANDISH

SCHOLASTIC BOOK SERVICES
New York Toronto London Auckland Sydney Tokyo

09-BTZ-101

Cover Photo by Herb Polsky

ISBN 0-590-31570-6

12 11 10 9 8 7 6 5 4 3 2 1   2   2 3 4 5 6 7/8

Printed in the U.S.A.   06

SOMEONE IS OUT THERE

A Windswept Book

WINDSWEPT TITLES
FROM SCHOLASTIC

CHAPTER 1

Christmas on Cape Cod?

Marcie Williams stared at her mother disbelievingly, and then shook her head so violently that her long, coppery hair swished about her shoulders.

"We can't!" she said. "We absolutely *can't!*"

Mrs. Williams's eyes widened as she looked at her daughter closely, her surprise at Marcie's reaction mixed with dismay.

"Grandmother Davies can't come to us," she pointed out.

"I *know* that," Marcie said. She frowned, then sudden tears glistened and she brushed them away impatiently as she moaned, "Oh, why did Grandmother have to fall and break her leg now?"

"This isn't like you, Marcie," Mrs. Williams said, her tone sharper. "You know perfectly well that my mother didn't break her leg on purpose!"

"Of course I do," Marcie conceded.

She sat down on the edge of one of the twin couches that flanked the walls in the Williams's spacious living room, quite unaware of the lovely

1

picture she made. She was wearing a plaid skirt in which green predominated, and her turtleneck sweater picked up the green tone. The color of her clothes made her eyes seem more green than hazel, and agitation had brought a flush to her cheeks that was actually very becoming.

She said, with a frankness that was disarming, "I know I'm acting like a selfish, spoiled brat. It's just that . . ."

Mrs. Williams picked up her crochet hook and yarn and started to work again on the lacy shawl she was making as a Christmas present for Grandmother Davies, but she paused briefly as Marcie's words trailed off. "Yes?" she asked.

"Well," Marcie said, "I counted on being here for the holidays. This *is* my senior year at Ashburton High, and I *am* class president. Also, do you realize this is the first time I've ever been in the same school for three years in a row in my whole life?"

"Yes, I do," Mrs. Williams said. "Your father and I both realize that having you and your brother changing schools so often has been difficult for you at times, but that's one of the penalties of being in the State Department's Foreign Service. We used to think about sending first Ben, and then you, to a boarding school, but we wanted you to grow up with us. Maybe it was selfish, but I don't think so. You've lived in many fascinating places, Marcie, and I think it has been more of an advantage than a disadvantage to both you and Ben. I can understand your feelings, though. Ashburton High, I know, is especially important to you."

"Yes, it is," Marcie said. "I've made a lot of friends in my class, real friends, and we're planning all sorts of things for the holidays. We're going to have a Christmas dance the night after school lets out, and Brad Evans has found a place out toward Frederick where you can actually rent a horse and sleigh. We're planning to have a sleigh-ride party, and that's just *one* of the things I can't wait for!"

"Marcie — "

"Also," Marcie continued hastily, "you know that Dr. Bardwell has asked me to do an independent study project, and that's quite an honor. I planned to start my research during the holidays."

"With all those parties going on?" Mrs. Williams asked, teasingly.

"Yes! Brad's going to help me, we're going to drive around all over the place. During the Civil War, there was a whole string of forts erected around Washington — in the District of Columbia itself, out here in Maryland, and in nearby Virginia. Brad says some of them have been restored, and you can find evidences of some of the others even now. I want to do my independent study project about them, and I've already started checking out the different locations."

"I see." Mrs. Williams had begun crocheting again, and her fingers flew as she said, with deceptive calm, "I was going to suggest that possibly you could do something in the area of

3

marine biology for the project. Cape Cod would make an ideal research site for anything like that."

"I don't know a thing about marine biology," Marcie said.

"I should think it would be quite a fascinating subject."

"Well, maybe it would be, but I've already told Dr. Bardwell what I plan to do," Marcie said. "He's approved the idea, and anyway, Mother, you know that marine biology wouldn't be my kind of thing."

"No, I don't necessarily know that, Marcie," Mrs. Williams said. "Is Brad Evans the real reason why you don't want to go to Cape Cod for Christmas?"

Marcie slid off the arm of the couch onto the couch itself and plumped two velvet pillows behind her head. She said thoughtfully, "I don't know. I honestly don't know. Brad's captain of the football team, he's very good-looking, and he's lots of fun to be with. Lately he's been trying to get me to make . . . well, to make sort of a commitment to him."

"What kind of commitment?" Mrs. Williams asked warily.

Marcie's eyes were direct as she gazed across at her mother. "Just to go steady," she said. "Nothing more than that. I'm not about to get into anything heavier. Not now. Not while I'm still in high school."

"Do you want to go steady with him?"

"I don't know." Marcie frowned. "Most of the

4

girls in my class would think I was flaking out if they knew I had any doubts about saying yes to Brad, but, much as I like him, I'm not sure I want to get serious with him. Like I said, he's a lot of fun, but sometimes it all seems to be on the surface. Do you know what I mean?"

"Yes," Mrs. Williams said, "I know what you mean."

Not for the first time, she was thankful for the spirit of frankness that existed between her daughter and herself. Her relationship with her son, Ben, had always been equally open, and thinking of him now she sighed.

"This is the first Christmas that Ben won't be home," she said. "I'm going to miss him dreadfully."

"So am I," Marcie said soberly. "Isn't there any way he could get a leave?"

"No. His aircraft carrier is in the Mediterranean, and they are not going to fly a young flight surgeon home for the holidays. The house will be very empty without him."

The tone of her mother's voice thoroughly captured Marcie's attention, and she began to feel as if she really were being "a selfish, spoiled brat."

She swallowed hard. "I'm sorry, Mother," she said simply. "I'll go to Cape Cod with you, without putting up any more arguments, and I'll do my best not to sulk!"

Marcie held to her promise; she even tried, that evening at dinner, to evince some enthusiasm for the upcoming holiday. Classes at Ashburton High would be over several days before Christmas, and the plan her parents evolved was that she and her mother would drive up to the Cape together, leaving Maryland as soon as school was dismissed at noon on the final day. They would drive as far as Delaware or New Jersey, stay in a motel overnight, and then go on to Cape Cod the following day. Mr. Williams planned to fly to the Cape Christmas Eve morning.

After dinner, Marcie tried to settle in and work on a history assignment, but it was impossible to concentrate. She was about to dial Brad Evans when she heard the telephone ringing, and her father called that it was for her. She took it on an extension in her parents' bedroom, curling up on the bed before she lifted the receiver off the hook.

She knew that she must tell Brad he should ask someone else to the Christmas dance and also find another date to take on the sleigh ride. Strangely, it didn't make her feel jealous to think of him going out with another girl. It was simply that she hated the thought of missing all the fun herself.

Regardless of her own feelings, though, Brad — who had been even more insistent about going steady than she had told her mother — was going to get pretty uptight at the thought of her going away for the holidays. It wasn't going to be easy to tell him about her family's plans, but it proved even harder than she expected.

"You're out of your tree!" Brad said bluntly.

"You've got to be putting me on! Cape Cod for Christmas?"

"That's right," Marcie said wearily, and prepared to try to explain it to him.

Cape Cod for Christmas.

CHAPTER 2

The weather had been bright and sunny all the way up the coast, but as they neared Cape Cod the skies became gray as if, Marcie thought, they sensed her feelings and wanted to match her mood.

All the way from Maryland, she and her mother had taken turns driving, and just now her mother was at the wheel. Staring out the window as they crossed a small bridge over a saltwater inlet, Marcie decided that the water was in on the conspiracy, too. It was lead gray, as were the wings of the gull that swooped down to perch atop a piling at the end of a rickety wooden pier.

"We're nearly at the bridge," Mrs. Williams said, and Marcie sensed an undercurrent of excitement in her mother's voice. It occurred to her, for the first time, that for her mother this was really coming home, in a way.

The house in Chatham where her grandmother lived had been in the Davies family for years. Growing up, her mother had spent all her summers there. About five years ago, Grandmother

Davies had decided to give up her apartment in New York and move to the Cape house permanently. It was an old house and had weathered many winters, and she said at the time that it was more truly her home than any other place on earth.

Marcie remembered it dimly. She had been to the Cape three times in her life, but she had been so young the first two times she didn't remember them at all. The third time had been when she was about eight. She recalled that you drove down a bumpy, sandy road to get to her grandmother's house, and that there was a beach right out in front of it. She and Ben had splashed through the water together, shouting as they doused each other.

That had been summer, though. There had been other children in houses that were reasonably nearby — no one lived "right next door" to her grandmother's place, as she remembered it — and she could recall playing with some of them, building sand castles and searching for different kinds of shells. Now those houses undoubtedly were closed, and when Marcie thought about the scene she was about to face only one word came to her mind: bleak.

They swung around a traffic circle and then started across the high, arching Sagamore Bridge, which spanned the Cape Cod Canal. There was a large freighter steaming through the Canal, and Marcie leaned forward to watch it.

The road to Grandmother Davies's house forked off Route 28 past the center of Chatham, and was every bit as long, sandy, and bumpy as Marcie had remembered.

Even her mother was daunted. As they jolted along, Mrs. Williams said, "I don't see how Mother ever gets in and out of here in really bad weather! She'd better stay put until that leg heals."

The house itself was gray-shingled, the original Cape Cod style house having been added on to many times in the past two centuries, so that there were all sorts of odd ells and angles.

Grandmother Davies's road was, in essence, a private lane. It dead-ended at her front door, and as her mother stopped the car, Marcie could glimpse, just beyond the house, the shimmer of gray water.

Gray. Was everything on Cape Cod gray?

A moment later she heard a voice with a flat, Cape Cod accent call out "They're here!" as the front door swung open.

The woman who stood in the doorway was nearly six feet tall, a gaunt woman with gray hair that had been combed straight back and twisted in a bun. She wore a brown woolen dress that reached nearly to her ankles, felt slippers, and a sweater with a hole in the front, and she was probably the homeliest woman Marcie had ever seen; but right now her New England austerity had been momentarily swept aside, and she was smiling broadly.

Mrs. Williams ran to her as if she were a child again and they hugged. Marcie followed more slowly, and her mother said, "Marcie, you remember Ella, don't you? This is Ella Mayo, Grandmother Davies's housekeeper."

"Yes, of course," Marcie said, and the memory of big, plump, molasses cookies came to her mind. Ella Mayo had always had cookies and milk waiting when she and Ben came in from the beach, that summer long ago.

Now the big, gaunt woman stood back and looked at her as if she couldn't believe her eyes. "Marcie!" she exclaimed. "You're all grown-up!"

"Yes, she is," Mrs. Williams agreed, but Marcie laughed.

"I'm not too grown-up to eat your molasses cookies," she told the housekeeper.

Ella's smile deepened. "I'll whip up a batch tomorrow," she promised.

"Constance! Marcie! Will you come on into the parlor? I can't get this blasted contraption going!"

It was Grandmother Davies, trying without success to get her wheelchair moving across the thick Oriental rug. It was brought back from the Far East long ago by her grandfather, who had been a sea captain.

Her leg, heavily encased in a plaster cast, was stretched out straight in front of her on a kind of platform, and she seemed rather pale; but her eyes were bright and she was obviously so happy to see them that Marcie very nearly started to cry.

Hugging and kissing her grandmother, she could not help but be ashamed of her reluctance to come to the Cape for Christmas. Being here, she realized now, *was* the most important thing,

11

a lot more important than the dances and parties back home and even more important than Brad Evans who, she knew, was considerably displeased with her for having gone along with her parents' plan.

"You *could* stay here with Trudy or one of our other friends over the holidays," he had pointed out to her, and for a moment, just a moment, she had thought about it. But then her answer had come, unbidden, even while he scowled at her.

"No," she had said, "I couldn't. I couldn't possibly! We've always been together at Christmas."

Now she was glad that she hadn't stayed in Maryland, as she settled down on a hassock near her grandmother, in front of the blazing wood fire. Ella brought tea and piping hot cranberry muffins with plenty of butter to spread on them, and as they talked — one taking up as the other left off, catching up on everything that had happened since they last met — Marcie forgot about the grayness that had been penetrating both her own spirit and the world just beyond the windows.

Later she unpacked, reveling in her room with its lovely old maple furniture, a patchwork quilt on the foot of the bed, and a braided rug, obviously hand-done, in the center of the floor. This was an old part of the house; the ceilings were so low that she realized Ben would have to duck as he came through the doorway, if he were here. The floor creaked slightly as she walked across it, but it was part of the charm of the old house. The house had atmosphere; it gave a person the feeling that there had been a lot of living within its walls. Obviously, this house had known a great deal of happiness, and also a great deal of sorrow, in its time.

Before dinner they had cold, tangy apple cider in front of the fireplace, and then Marcie pushed her grandmother's wheelchair into the dining room and settled her in at her place at the head of the table.

The dining room was wallpapered in blue, and there were shelves lined with lovely old china and pewter, which gleamed softly in the candlelight. Ella had made crisp clam fritters, and with them went baked beans and cole slaw and hot corn bread.

"Real Cape Cod food," she told them as she served it. "I wanted you two to get right in the swing of things here!"

After dinner, Marcie helped Ella wash the dishes, despite the housekeeper's initial protests, and then she joined her mother and her grandmother in front of the fire. She soon grew sleepy, however, and her grandmother said, smiling, "It's the salt air. You have to get accustomed to it."

Upstairs, opening her bedroom window, Marcie really could smell the tang of salt in the air. The wind that blew across her cheeks was chilly and had a clammy touch to it.

There was no moon tonight, and no visible stars. It was a very dark world outside, and Marcie shivered slightly as she left the window open just a crack and climbed into bed. The patchwork quilt looked so inviting that she unfolded it and spread it over herself, letting its coziness envelop her. She turned out the light in the old flower-patterned china lamp on her bedside table, and almost at once she fell asleep.

CHAPTER 3

Marcie had never been a late sleeper, so she was amazed when, slowly awakening, she looked at her wristwatch and saw that it was nearly nine o'clock.

She dressed quickly, choosing warm slacks and a sweater, and went downstairs to find Ella in the kitchen, already beginning to "whip up" the promised batch of molasses cookies.

Ella only laughed when Marcie protested about having slept too late. "You needed that sleep," she told her. "Change of climate always affects a person. Your mother and your grandmother are having a second cup of coffee in the parlor. Just wait a second till I get this batter together, and I'll fix you some bacon and eggs."

"I'm going to gain ten pounds while I'm here if I don't watch it," Marcie said, when she had finished the bacon, the eggs, and some of yesterday's warmed-up cranberry muffins.

"Wouldn't hurt you if you did," Ella said.

"Yes, it would," Marcie assured her. "Nothing I own would fit!"

She looked out the kitchen window. There was

15

a stretch of stubbly lawn, then just beyond it the water, which today had the deep gray sheen of the pewter in Grandmother Davies's dining room. The sky was oyster in color; the whole effect was depressing. Marcie sighed. The day stretched ahead of her, *all* the days of her holiday stretched ahead of her, and there seemed to be very little she could do with them. Much as she loved both her mother and her grandmother, she couldn't just sit in front of the fireplace talking to them forever.

She said, "I think I'll go for a walk."

"Nasty out," said Ella. "Why don't you curl up with a book? Plenty of books in those cases in the back parlor."

"Maybe I will, later, but right now I need some exercise," Marcie said.

"Then bundle up," Ella advised, "and put something over your hair. They don't call Chatham the 'fog factory' of the Cape for nothing, and if that fog starts rolling in you'll find it seems wetter than water."

Marcie had brought a warm quilted parka with her. It seemed almost too warm as she slipped into it, but, once she was out of the house and walking along the beach, she realized that Ella had been right. The damp chill in the air penetrated; she unzipped the hood and covered her hair with it, buttoning it under her chin.

Grandmother Davies owned a fairly large section of beachfront, so there was quite a distance between her house and the next one that faced the water. As Marcie had suspected, both that

16

house and the one beyond it were closed up. Wooden shutters had been nailed over the windows to protect them from the winds of winter, and this gave them an air of what seemed to Marcie an almost appalling loneliness. There was, in fact, a kind of total desolation to the whole scene that made her feel increasingly homesick for Maryland and her friends there.

This was not the open ocean along here, but rather a wide, saltwater bay called Pleasant Bay. You had to cross the bay and then the sandy barrier that fringed it to the east before you came to the broad Atlantic itself.

It was tidal water, though, and just now the tide was low. The sand flats shimmered with a beige gray of their own, strewn here and there with clumps of seaweed, shells, and the flotsam of bottles and miscellany left over from summer. Marcie saw a child's small, bright blue plastic truck and one pink beach sandal, and she wondered where their owners were now.

Today the bay did not look at all "pleasant," she decided. It looked, in fact, icy and sullen and she had the odd sense that she was an intruder.

Well, she thought, trudging on through the sand, she *didn't* belong here. No matter how pleasant it had been at the house last night, no matter how good it was to see Grandmother Davies's happiness at having some of her family with her, Cape Cod in winter was not Marcie's kind of place, and that was all there was to it!

The sand, having become thoroughly chilled over the weeks of fall and early winter, was packed down. It crunched beneath her feet, and it was much easier to walk on than a summer beach. As she rounded a point, Marcie realized she had come quite a distance and was about to turn back, when she was brought up short by the sight of a small, ramshackle wooden cabin. It was nestled in the shelter of the outcropping of dunes that had begun a way back and were steadily getting higher.

For a long moment, she stood very still. There was something about the cabin that almost frightened her. It wasn't even a cabin, really; it was not much more than a shack. A single window gaped in the center of rough shingles that had been nailed in an irregular fashion, one over the other, with a view only toward enclosing something. There was none of the neat precision one saw on most of the Cape's well-shingled houses. Surprisingly, the window had not been shuttered in preparation for winter. The glass, though, seemed covered with a coating, probably from the salt air, that made it almost opaque.

Though Marcie doubted if she could see very much of the inside of the shack even if she were to go closer to the window and peer in, she wondered if there might be someone inside, even now, looking out at her.

It was a disquieting thought and she nearly turned around to start back on the long trek to her grandmother's house. But it was equally disturbing to think of turning her back on the window without knowing whether or not someone was watching her. The very thought, in fact, sent shivers of fear tingling up and down her spine.

Possibly, she thought, if she walked closer to the tide line she could glance sideways toward the shack and catch any sign of color or movement. This she did, only to discover that the side of the building facing the water was blank, with just a haphazard pattern of shingles and no windows at all.

No one could see her from this angle either, she told herself, so she kept on going until she had passed the shack. Then she turned around because those strange sensations were coursing up and down her back again.

There was a single window on the other side, and next to it, toward the water, there was a door. It was a heavy wooden door, which seemed as lopsided in its way as the shingles. A big, stone slab served as a doorstep.

Marcie paused, and it seemed to her as if the entire world suddenly was standing still. Before, she had been conscious of the faint sound of water lapping against the sand; now even that had stopped. Earlier, she had heard the cry of a seagull, but now, although she would have welcomed either the sound or the sight of a gull, the sky was empty.

It was empty except for a deepening mist that not only was coming closer but seemed literally to be reaching out toward her, a pale gray ethereal octopus with clutching fingers. Fog.

Never before in her life had Marcie felt so alone, but as she realized this she also became sure of something else. She *was* alone. The shack was empty. If it hadn't been, certainly the occupant would have shown himself or herself by now, unless some sort of hermit lived in the place, and she doubted this. Although the site seemed lonely enough in December, certainly during the summer there would be people all along the beachfront and boats and water-skiers out in Pleasant Bay. She could remember that Ben had water-skied with friends that summer they visited her grandmother. This would be no place for a hermit during Cape Cod's summer season!

The thought of this gave her courage. Probably, she told herself, the shack was used by some fisherman, maybe only on a part-time basis when he happened to be working out of Chathamport, which was where her mother had said the fishing boats brought their catches. She didn't know much about fishermen, but it seemed perfectly possible that they could fish from different places, and perhaps sometimes one had better luck one place than another.

Even as she decided this, Marcie found herself walking slowly toward the shack.

She tried to tell herself that she had absolutely no right to trespass, but she knew perfectly well that was what she was going to do — unless she opted for logic instead of curiosity and went back home where she belonged. Even though she knew that was what she *should* do, her curiosity was getting the upper hand.

Now that she was convinced — well, *almost*

convinced — that there was no one inside, what possible harm could it do to just peek in the window?

She edged toward the window, almost laughing out loud at herself because she knew she must look like a crab, moving across the sand sideways. She went to the base of the dunes, keeping a wide distance between herself and the door to the shack, and it was only now that she noticed a flight of rickety steps leading up to the top of the dunes. They were so weatherbeaten that they blended in perfectly with the gray of the day, and the beige of the sand and beach grass.

This, then, must be the way the occupant of the shack went in and out, for obviously it would be a long walk all the way around the point, either toward her grandmother's house or toward the homes that might be farther along this side. Also, it would be a steep climb up and down the dunes. It would be difficult, Marcie thought, to get a firm footing in the jutting outcroppings of tangled vines, withered leaves, and the spiky branches of bare bushes; and the bare sandy patches would be shifting and slippery.

Now she more than half-feared that someone might suddenly loom up at the top of the steps, and it wasn't a very pleasant idea.

The fog was thickening. She could still see through it — it wasn't that dense — but the thought of suddenly being trapped in a fog that you couldn't see through spurred Marcie into action.

She slipped quickly across to the window and peered in, and was rewarded by a view of . . . nothing! The window panes were obviously covered with grime on the inside and salt spray on the outside, and this gave them as effective a coating as if they had been painted over.

Marcie didn't stop to think. She moved along the side of the house to the wide stone step and pushed gently at the door. To her surprise and growing horror, it began to swing inward with a screeching sound that set her on edge. She felt certain that if there were anyone within miles they would hear it!

She had not intended to go this far, to actually go inside the shanty, but again curiosity won out over common sense. She put one foot and then the other inside the door and found herself standing in the middle of a small, very grubby room. A bunk bed at the far side was heaped with rumpled sheets and blankets, and a pillow still bore the faint imprint of someone's head.

A musty smell assailed her. It was the peculiar, damp odor of a place near salt water that has been unoccupied for a time, mixed with mildew and something she suspected was decaying food.

It seemed obvious that it had been a long while since the dirty windows had been opened, or since any fresh air at all had swept through the shack, or since the person who had last used the bed had lived here.

Spiders had taken over the corners of the room, and there was a regular network of cobwebs. Cobwebs also interlaced the rungs of a straight chair pushed under a table, which looked as if it had been used as a makeshift desk. There was a cardboard carton stashed beneath the table, filled with papers and some ledgers. On top of the table-desk there was a pad of blank paper, a couple of ballpoint pens, and a lamp.

Marcie flicked the light switch on the lamp, but it didn't go on. The electricity had been turned off, which further proved to her that it was a long time since anyone had lived here.

She went on into the small kitchen at the back of the shack. Shelves had been built into one corner, and she noticed that there was quite a good supply of canned goods lining them. There were dirty dishes in the sink, which came as no surprise at this point, but she wrinkled her nose at the smell that emanated from them. A small refrigerator stood in another corner; she opened the door and recoiled from the foul odor. There was ground meat — obviously spoiled long ago — soured milk, and two or three rotten tomatoes.

She closed the refrigerator door swiftly and turned to the stained, two-burner stove. An enamelware coffee pot stood on one of the burners, and she lifted the lid to become aware of yet another in this dreadful combination of odors; the pot was about half-full of coffee, its surface covered with a scum of green mold.

She was just replacing the pot lid when, her fingers still grasping it, she was suddenly swept by the strong sensation that she was no longer alone. She knew she was being watched — this time it wasn't imagination!

She turned to see the menacing figure of a man filling the kitchen doorway, and his voice rang out.

"What do you think you're doing?" he demanded angrily.

CHAPTER 4

There was no place to retreat to. Marcie, trying not to cringe, swirled to face the accuser, who was advancing upon her. He stopped short, staring at her.

She, in turn, stared back at him.

He was certainly not the ogre he had appeared to be, when that first glimpse of him in silhouette had made him seem a singularly menacing figure. He was, in fact, one of the handsomest boys she had ever seen!

He was tall, just about as tall as her brother Ben, she would guess, and Ben was a couple of inches over six feet. He wore black rubber knee boots and a bright yellow rubberized jacket that reminded her of paintings she had seen of New England fishermen. There was a hood to his jacket which he had thrown back over his shoulders, and his light brown hair was wind-rumpled. One lock kept falling forward over his forehead, and he pushed it back impatiently as he scowled at her.

Even though it was winter, he was deeply suntanned, and Marcie decided that never before in her life had she seen eyes so intensely blue. Just now they were glacial as he surveyed her and asked again, his tone more cold than furious this time, "What are you doing here?"

She had never felt so foolish! Her cheeks began to sting, and she knew she must actually be blushing, although she surely had never considered herself the blushing type.

"Nothing," she said.

"Come on, now," he said scornfully. "People don't pry into other people's places without a reason. Who are you, anyway?"

Marcie could imagine how her mother, her grandmother, and Ella would react if they learned she actually had been poking around on someone else's property. She said quickly, mustering all the self-control she could, "It doesn't matter. Look, I'm sorry. I didn't realize anyone lived here. I thought the place was just abandoned. I'll leave right now."

Despite his good looks, Marcie didn't like the expression that came into his eyes; because he was young and handsome it didn't mean that he couldn't also be dangerous, she warned herself. She wished desperately that the shack had a back door she could escape through to get away from him.

As it was, she could only try to slip by him quickly and hope that once she got outside the fog would be thick enough that she could run into it and vanish from his sight.

Marcie was quick, but she was not quick

enough. As she moved toward the door he shot out one arm and grabbed her.

"Not so fast!" he told her.

She put every ounce of strength she possessed into twisting out of his grip and literally careened past him, tearing through the room where the bunk bed and the table were and out the front door. She was unprepared for the rough surface of the stone slab that served as a doorstep, though. She stumbled, catapulted out onto the sand and beach grass just beyond, and landed face down.

In an instant, he was beside her. The fog was thickening. In fact, it was getting so thick that she knew she might have eluded him if she had managed to start running. She felt a twinge in her ankle, and that really did it! Despite herself, she cried out.

"You're hurt!" she heard him exclaim. "Hey, turn over, will you, and let me see what you've done to yourself?"

She struggled to a sitting position, wanting very much to rub her aching ankle but determined not to do so, because she didn't want him to know that she might not be able to run at all, that maybe the best thing she could do was limp!

He had crouched down very close to her, and his blue eyes were regarding her with what could only be termed real anxiety.

He said, "I'm sorry. Honestly, I *am* sorry. I must have given you the devil of a scare."

"You . . . you did," she admitted.

He smiled wryly. "Well," he said, "you gave

me something of a scare yourself." He gestured over his shoulder, toward the shack. "I was pretty startled to find someone inside there," he confessed. "What *were* you doing? Will you tell me now?"

"Well," Marcie said, avoiding the intensity of those blue eyes, "I suppose my grandmother's housekeeper would say I was poking my nose where it had no business."

"Who is your grandmother's housekeeper?"

"Ella Mayo."

He laughed. "You're right, then. I'm sure Miss Mayo would tell you that you were minding anything but your own business!"

Marcie had never considered herself the crying type any more than she considered herself the blushing type. Now she knew that tears were much too close to the surface, and she was determined not to cry in front of him.

"I didn't mean any harm," she murmured.

"Yes," he said drily, "I *will* say that you don't look like most people's concept of the average thief or intruder. If I may say so, Mrs. Davies's granddaughter, it's pretty foolish to go into a place when you don't even know who or what may be there."

He had called her Mrs. Davies's granddaughter! "You know my grandmother?" Marcie asked him, surprised.

"Yes. I know both your grandmother and Ella Mayo. Chatham, off season, is still a relatively small place."

Marcie started to get up, but then she winced

and slumped down again. Immediately he said anxiously, "You *did* hurt yourself when you flew out like that."

"I've twisted my ankle," she admitted morosely.

"Well, let's see if you can stand on it at all," he said.

He stood first and reached down for her, and she felt herself being drawn upright by two very strong arms. He held her tight for a long moment, the fog swirling about both of them, and she had the crazy feeling that she wouldn't mind in the least if he just kept on holding her for a while.

She took a tentative step and then another, and he said, "Well, that's good. At least you haven't gone and broken a bone or anything."

"That would be the final disaster right now," Marcie said. "Grandmother Davies already has her leg in a cast. We don't need another invalid around the house."

"Yes," he said. "It really was too bad about your grandmother. I've been meaning to stop by and see her. How is she doing?"

"All right," Marcie said, "but it's going to take quite a while before her leg is any good to her again."

She was hobbling along with his assistance as she spoke, and he said, "Look, this may sound crazy to you, but I'm going to hoist you across to the doorstep and then let's take your shoes off, okay?"

"What?"

"I said it may sound crazy, but I want you to

wade out in the water, just for a minute or so. It will be icy; it will have the same effect as putting ice on that ankle. It will help keep the swelling down. In case you don't realize it, Mrs. Davies's granddaughter, the first thing you should do in the case of most injuries of this kind is to apply cold."

Before she could protest, he swooped her off her feet, and a moment later she had her shoes off and her slacks rolled up to mid-calf.

"The tide's coming in," he told her. "I'm going to carry you out to where your ankle will be covered, and then we'll let you stand in the water just long enough for the cold to do it some good."

"But what about you?" she asked.

"My feet, you mean?" He gestured to his boots. "They're totally waterproof."

Although Marcie was a sturdy girl, he picked her up as if she were quite an easy burden. Again she had the feeling that she wouldn't mind being held in his arms for a long time.

The first touch of the icy water on her ankles very nearly made her scream, but she gritted her teeth and bore it. When he had carried her back to the stone step again and was helping her get her socks and shoes on, he said, "I've got to hand it to you. I think I would have yelled."

"I almost did."

"It's that sturdy New England stock," he said. "If you are Mrs. Davies's granddaughter, obviously you come from it." He rocked back on his heels. "Are you going to make me call you Mrs. Davies's granddaughter forever?" he demanded.

"What? Oh," Marcie said, "my name is Marcie Williams."

His smile seemed to lighten the fog. "I'm Peter Doane," he told her.

Peter Doane. She liked the sound of it. Only one thing troubled her. She could not understand his connection with this beach shack that was not much more than a hovel, when you got right down to it. Why had *he* come here? Did he actually ever live in this place?

She asked, tentatively, "Do you live in Chatham all year round?"

She noticed that he hesitated for a moment before he answered her. Then he said, "Yes. Yes, I do."

She had to come out with it. "Here?" she asked him.

"Here?" he echoed, puzzled. "Oh, you mean, in this shack? No." It was a quick, sharp negative. "I've been out clamming, and I . . . I stopped by here on an errand, on the way home. This place belonged to my uncle's partner."

Belonged? He obviously was not inclined to say anything further, and something warned her not to pursue it. Also, whatever errand he had come on was still unfulfilled; finding her in the shack had put a stop to it. Was he going to complete it now, whatever it was?

Evidently not. He made this clear when he said, "The fog's getting thicker and the tide's coming in. I think we'd better start walking toward your grandmother's house, if you think you can. It's going to hurt, I know. I left my

31

uncle's truck up on the street back of here and came across the dunes, but I think the steps and the walk over the top would almost be harder for you than just going along the beach."

He had been clamming, he was using his uncle's truck, and this grimy shack had belonged to his uncle's partner. Marcie could think of a dozen questions she wanted to ask him but she posed only one.

"Where are the clams?"

They had started walking, moving slowly, the fog so dense now that they could see only a few feet in front of them, but he stopped short and peered down at her.

"What?"

"You said you'd been clamming. I just asked you where the clams are, or didn't you get any?"

"Yes, as a matter of fact, I got a lot, which will please my aunt because she wants to make a chowder," he said. "I left the clams in the truck."

"Oh." She was trying not to sound too inquisitive, even though she was bursting with curiosity about him. "I thought," she said, waving vaguely in the direction of the water, "that maybe you'd been clamming out there. It *was* low tide, and that *is* when you go clamming, isn't it?"

"Yes," he said gravely, "it *was* low tide and that *is* when you go clamming." She had the feeling that he was laughing at her, but it was a gentle kind of laughter. "However, I have a secret spot farther on up the bay, a couple of miles from here, and that's where I went. I live with my aunt and uncle, and my uncle and I are both commercial fishermen. Is that what you wanted to know?"

It was her turn to stop, in sheer surprise. "You're a *fisherman?*" she demanded, incredulously.

"Yes," he said drily. "Is that so strange?"

"Well, yes," she said. "I mean, I don't know. I mean, you don't *look* . . ."

"I don't look like a fisherman?"

"No, you don't," Marcie said, wishing that she had never opened her mouth on the subject. "I mean, well, I guess the fishermen you see in pictures are always grizzled old men in bright yellow coats."

"We call it foul-weather gear," he said, his voice curiously expressionless. "So, I fit your mental picture only in regard to the yellow coat, is that it?" He was not looking at her now, he was staring out into the fog. He said, "As for the old and grizzled part of it, some of the fishermen you see, even in pictures, are not nearly as old as you might think. The sea can age a man very quickly, Marcie."

He spoke very soberly, and suddenly he seemed much older himself.

Marcie said hesitantly, feeling her way, painfully aware of her ignorance about those men who followed the sea and tried to wrest a living from it. "Do you fish even in winter?"

"Yes," he told her. "We didn't go out today—the weather was too poor and our boat isn't equipped the way it should be." There was a bitterness to the way he said this. "We fish all

33

year round, though. Some of the larger boats go out for days at a time. The big trawlers go to fish off the Georges Bank, which is one of the major fishing grounds in the world. Maybe you've heard about the Russians and the Germans and people from other countries fishing there. There has been quite a lot of trouble about it, in years past."

"No," Marcie admitted, "I really haven't heard about it. I suppose maybe I'm not as well informed about a lot of things as I might be," she added, although she had never thought about it in quite this light before. "I've been away from the States for long periods of time during most of my life," she explained.

"Oh?"

"My father's a Foreign Service officer. He's been stationed at American embassies in different parts of the world. It's almost like being in the Army or Navy, except that you don't wear a uniform."

"I know what the diplomatic service is, Marcie," he said, an edge of sarcasm to his voice. "Even we fishermen read the newspapers once in a while."

"Peter . . ." she began.

"Yes?"

"Well, you're getting entirely the wrong impression," Marcie said staunchly. "I suppose what I should come right out and say is that I don't know very much about commercial fishing, and I guess there are many things about my own country that have sort of passed me by because I've been away from it so much."

"I see," he said gravely.

They walked in silence for a moment. Then he asked, "How's the ankle?"

"It really doesn't feel too bad," Marcie said. "You were right about the cold water. It helped, though it seemed like pretty rough treatment at the time."

He laughed. "I'm sure it did."

A shape loomed through the fog; Marcie saw that it was the first of the shuttered summer houses and knew they were nearing her grandmother's place. She wondered if he would come inside and have a cup of coffee or something, if she invited him. She was surprised at how much she wanted to see him again, but she sensed that even though he might feel the same way, it was very likely he was going to drop her at her door and let it go at that.

It had been stupid of her, she told herself savagely, to say "You're a *fisherman?*" in that totally surprised tone of voice, a tone that had made it seem as if she didn't think much of people who made their living commercial fishing all year round.

Peter interrupted her thoughts by asking, "Where do you live now, Marcie?"

"In Bethesda, Maryland," she said, "right outside Washington."

"Are you going to be in Chatham long?"

Hope surged; maybe he *was* going to ask if he could see her again after all. "Through the Christmas holidays," she told him, the words tumbling out. "That is, we'll be here till after New Year's. It's just my mother and I, right now, but my father will be joining us Christmas Eve."

They had passed the second of the shuttered houses; now the next house along the beach front would be her grandmother's.

Peter said, "That will be great for your grandmother. I'm sure it would be very lonely for her this Christmas, especially, without any family around."

That was it. That was all.

Marcie tried to fight down her obvious disappointment as they came to her door and he courteously declined her offer to come in.

"I've really got to get back to the truck and take those clams home," he told her. "Later on, you might take a good hot bath and soak that ankle. Ella Mayo can tell you better than I can, but the remedy is cold at first, followed later by heat."

"Yes," she said. "Yes, I'll do that."

He turned, and she watched him helplessly, knowing that in another minute he would stride away and be swallowed up by the fog. He lifted his hand, as if to wave good-bye, then he paused and came back to her.

"Marcie," he said, "one more thing. Don't go back to that beach shack. Don't go *near* it again, okay? When you want to take a walk along the beach, head in the other direction."

With that he was gone.

Had he been voicing an order because the

cabin belonged to his uncle's partner, or had he been warning her away from it for some much more sinister reason? Marcie, looking after him, had the sinking feeling that it was the latter.

CHAPTER 5

Marcie, limping into the house, told her grandmother, her mother, and Ella only that she had stumbled and fallen while she was out walking. Actually this was the truth, if not the entire truth, but for reasons that she couldn't explain even to herself she didn't want, just now, to bring up her encounter with Peter.

Ella had made a rich fish chowder for lunch, and they had grapenut custard pudding and some of the big, fat molasses cookies Marcie had always remembered. Afterwards she played cribbage with her grandmother and then, Ella having told her the same thing Peter had told her, she went upstairs and ran a hot bath, sprinkled herbal beads into the water, and tried to relax as she soaked her foot.

She was uptight, though, because of Peter's final remark; *definitely* it had been a warning. In fact, it seemed almost like a threat.

Why should he be so anxious that she stay away from the shack?

Ella had told her to get off her feet for a while, and had gone so far as to suggest that a nap

would be the best thing for her on a damp, fo
afternoon like this one. Marcie put on her yell
wool robe and snuggled down on the bed with
the patchwork quilt drawn over her. She tried to
think of what there could possibly be about the
grubby little shack that would make it important
for her to keep away from it.

If it were being used for any sort of illegal
purposes it would surely have shown signs of
more recent occupation. Cobwebs could appear
quickly, though, and food would spoil without
refrigeration, even in cool weather. She had no
idea how long it might take to grow a layer of
mold on cold coffee, and wished now that she
had taken more interest in her science subjects in
school. As it was, history fascinated her, as did
the law. Her very first year of high school, when
she took a course in government, she had decided that she wanted to be a lawyer one day.

After dinner that night, Marcie — trying to
mask the limp her ankle was causing — insisted
that her foot was fine, and she followed Ella into
the kitchen after the housekeeper had cleared
the table.

Over Ella's protests, she said that she would
dry the dishes as they were washed, and the
housekeeper, obviously pleased despite her as-
sumed gruffness about the matter, finally handed
her a strawberry-patterned dish towel.

Peter knew Ella Mayo, which meant, of course,
that Ella also knew Peter; Marcie was posi-
tive that Ella must know Peter's aunt and uncle,
too, as well as the partner who either owned, or

had owned, the beach shack. Marcie suspected there wasn't too much of interest that transpired around Chatham that Ella Mayo wouldn't know about, except maybe things that involved the summer people.

She was conscious that Ella was watching her closely, and the housekeeper said, "You aren't fooling me, Marcie! That ankle's still paining you. You ought to be off it!"

"I'll go to bed as soon as we finish cleaning up," Marcie promised. She hesitated, wondering just how to go about this. Then she decided that the best approach was a direct approach.

"Ella," she said, "you know that old shack down the beach? It's around the point, under the dunes."

Ella stopped midway through washing a blue-and-white china platter. "Yes," she said. "What about it?"

"Who owns it?"

Ella rinsed the platter, put it aside, and dried her hands on a towel before she answered. She gave Marcie a long look, and Marcie's heart sank. Ella's face, she thought, looked like a blank wall.

"What do you want to know for?" Ella asked her, her accent flatter than ever.

"Well," Marcie said, "I walked down that far this morning, and I wondered about it."

The housekeeper's eyes were blue, too — not a deep, indescribable blue like Peter's eyes — but a very pale shade. They were also, Marcie realized uncomfortably, very, very sharp.

"Marcie Williams," Ella said sternly, "did you go poking around that shack?"

Marcie put down the dish towel she had been holding, and she could feel her lips trembling. "Yes," she admitted, faltering beneath Ella's accusing gaze. "Yes, I'm afraid I did."

"You had no mind to!" Ella nearly snapped at her.

"But why not?" Marcie protested. "I didn't intend to do any harm. I was just . . . curious."

"Seems to me," Ella said curtly, "that you're old enough to know the trouble curiosity can get a person into."

"Yes, I suppose I am," Marcie acknowledged. "I don't know . . . the shack just sort of fascinated me. So I tried to see through the window . . ."

"Yes," Ella prompted her.

"Well . . . I pushed the door and it opened."

The housekeeper was horrified. "You mean to say you went *inside*?"

"Yes," Marcie said. "Yes, I did."

"Marcie, Marcie!" Ella's face was no longer a blank wall — her agitation was thoroughly visible. "You'd no *mind* to do a thing like that!" She swallowed hard, she looked taller and more gaunt than ever. She said, forcing the words, "There was murder done!"

Marcie recoiled, actually moving back a step or two. Her eyes were fixed on the housekeeper's face, and there was pure horror in her voice.

"You mean," she asked, "someone was *murdered* in the shack?"

"Not *in* the shack," Ella said impatiently.

"Atop the dunes right back of it. There's a path across from the street."

"Who . . . who was it?" Marcie asked in a whisper.

"Wouldn't matter to you," Ella said, and then tried to turn her attention back to the dishes. "No one you'd know," she said, as she turned on the hot water again. "Just gave me a start, that's all, when you said you went inside his place."

Ella began to wash an old, hand-painted butter dish. She said, her back turned to Marcie, "Don't ever go down that way again, Marcie. There's nothing good about that shack!"

Marcie shook her head despairingly. "You're saying just what Peter Doane told me, though in a slightly different way," she accused.

The butter dish was put down, and Ella again dried her hands and turned around.

"What *about* Peter Doane?" she asked sharply, and again there was that blank wall look on her face.

"He came into the shack when I was there," Marcie stammered. "That's how I happened to twist my ankle. I was trying to run away from Peter."

"Trying to run away from *Peter?*" Ella echoed incredulously.

"Yes. At first, that was. Later, it was . . . different." Marcie looked at the housekeeper imploringly. "Ella," she asked, "who is Peter? And who owned the beach shack? And why was he murdered?"

She felt as if Ella's pale blue eyes were probing

right into her brain, but finally the housekeeper nodded. "All right," she decided, "we've nearly done washing up. I'll finish a bit later." She walked over to the kitchen table and drew out a chair, motioning to Marcie to do the same. They sat across from each other, and Ella said unhappily, "Wish this had never come up."

"I'm sorry, Ella," Marcie said. "That is," she added honestly, "I'm sorry about the shack. I can't say I'm sorry I met Peter."

"It would be as well if you hadn't," said the housekeeper.

"Why?" Marcie asked, and was almost afraid of the answer.

"'Tisn't Peter himself," Ella said shortly. "It's everything around him. Peter's uncle, name's Willis Higgins, is a fisherman. Lived here all his life, he has; his father was a fisherman before him. May Higgins, his wife, is Peter's aunt. May and Peter's mother were sisters. May's a smart one; teaches science at Chatham High School. Peter takes after her — natural enough, I guess, because she brought him up through some pretty important years."

"He said he lived with his uncle and aunt," Marcie remembered.

"Yes. Has since he was twelve years old. His parents were both killed in a terrible accident. Just before Christmas, it was, right this time of year. They lived in Connecticut, and they were coming down to the Cape to spend Christmas with Willis and May.

"Peter was in the car with them, but he was

thrown clear. He was hurt pretty bad at the time. May brought him home with her once he was out of the hospital, and ever since then he's been almost like the son she never had."

Marcie swallowed hard. There had been an odd, almost wistful, note in Peter's voice when he spoke about how her grandmother would have been lonely at Christmas without any family around. The memory of this wistfulness, now that she knew his story, made her feel as if she could cry for him, even though she strongly suspected that this was the last thing Peter Doane would want her to do.

She said, "That's so sad, Ella."

"Yes." The housekeeper nodded. "Yes, 'tis sad. Peter has had a lot of bad knocks, for someone young as he is. He could be bitter, he could take off like a lot of the young people into drink or drugs, and you couldn't blame him as much as you can most because he'd have a good reason. He's got character, though. He's going to come through all right."

Marcie posed the question carefully. "Obviously you think a lot of him, Ella. If that's so, why do you say it would have been better if I hadn't met him?"

"It was Peter I was thinking of, not you," Ella said, bluntly, yet with a gentleness that was rare for her. "The boy's had more than his share, and you're a very pretty girl. It wouldn't do for him to get smitten with you, not at this time in his life."

44

"Ella," Marcie said, trying to laugh. "Aren't you rushing things?"

"Things sometimes don't take much rushing," Ella countered. "You get a look on your face when you talk about Peter Doane, and it seems to me that could be the beginning of something he shouldn't take on. Not now. He's got more than enough on his plate."

The question had to be asked. "Ella," Marcie ventured, "what connection is there between Peter and the beach shack and the murder?"

Ella came close to putting on her blank wall look again, then relented. "'Twas a man named Howard Flynn who was murdered. He was an old bachelor, an old crab, if you ask my opinion. He lived in that shack year round. He was Willis Higgins's partner. They owned the *May-Bee* together — she's a long-line fishing boat out of Chathamport."

Ella paused, sighing. "Never did know why Willis and Howard Flynn ever got tied up with each other in the first place. Everyone's always liked Willis, but no one, to my mind, ever liked Howard. Guess it was a matter of money. Neither of 'em had enough to swing a boat alone, so they pooled together.

"That was quite a while back, and the *May-Bee* was in pretty good shape when they bought her, but even then she needed some repairs. You can be sure it was Willis, not Howard, who did anything that was needed to be done. Later on, when equipment began to break down, 'twas always a fight to get Howard to agree to put his share toward replacing it."

Marcie remembered that Peter had said he and his uncle didn't go out to fish in bad weather, because their boat wasn't as well equipped as it should be.

"Why wouldn't this Howard Flynn keep up his share of things?" she asked Ella.

"He was like one of them real misers you read about," Ella said. "He socked it away, that's what. My one satisfaction," she said, "may the Lord forgive me," and her face actually creased into a smile, "is that he couldn't take it with him!"

Marcie almost smiled herself, but her thoughts went back to Peter.

"Who murdered Howard Flynn?" she asked the housekeeper.

"That's just it," Ella said glumly. "They haven't found out. Wouldn't surprise me if they never do, and that keeps a cloud hanging right over Willis, which means there's a cloud hanging over Peter, too. Peter's never apt to forget that his uncle took him in after his parents were killed, and finished bringing him up. Willis helped the best he could, too, toward Peter's going off to college."

"Peter was in college?" Marcie asked. "What happened? Did he drop out?"

"Yes." Ella nodded. "He felt he had to drop out. His uncle needed help, so this past fall Peter didn't go-back. He was studying at the University of Rhode Island. He wants to be a marine biologist, and May told me they got a very good program in marine biology there. She was so excited when Peter was accepted into it."

"How long was he there?"

"Well, let's see. Peter's twenty-one now, was twenty-one last month, matter of fact. He worked for a year after high school to build up his bank account. He's had two years at the university, and the pity is, he did so well they gave him a scholarship that would have paid most of his expenses the rest of the time."

"Then why did his aunt let him drop out?" Marcie protested. "It seems so wrong!"

"Well," Ella said reasonably, "sometimes you got a duty that has to come first, Marcie. Peter felt his first duty was to Willis. It was Willis who was the main suspect in Howard Flynn's murder. He nearly got arrested for it, matter of fact. I hear that Tim Bearse — he's the Chief of Police — still swears Willis did it, and that one of these days he'll have enough evidence to prove it. Like I told you, it's put a real cloud over Willis, it's taken its toll on him. I've never seen a man age so much in as short a time."

"How long ago did the murder happen?"

"Last August," Ella said tersely. Her pale eyes had a faraway look as she remembered it. "We had a near brush from a hurricane coming up the coast," she recalled. "Veered off to sea before it reached the Cape, it did. Wasn't much real damage done, just some tree limbs blown down. It hit the power lines in a few places so we were without electricity for a while. They fix things up fast these days, though. In the old times, I remember being without power for a week or ten days, sometimes, after a big storm."

Ella sighed, and Marcie sensed that she really didn't want to talk about the murder. She fought to restrain her impatience, and finally the house-keeper continued.

"Like always, when there are storm warnings posted, the fishermen worry about their boats," she said. "Not without good reason, either. If a boat isn't secured properly it can be battered to pieces in gale force winds, to say nothing of hurricane winds, which are a lot stronger.

"Usually, it was Willis who went to look after the *May-Bee* whenever there were storm warnings, not Howard," Ella said. It was pretty obvious, Marcie thought, that her grandmother's housekeeper had not liked Willis Higgins's partner.

"That day, though," Ella went on, " 'twas Howard who went down to the fish pier, because Willis had wrenched his back. He wasn't really laid up with it, but he wasn't supposed to lift and haul things, and that's part of a fisherman's life.

"Anyway, Howard went down to the pier and did what needed to be done with the boat. Some of the other fishermen were down there at the time; later they mentioned they'd talked to him. Said he seemed like he always did, which was on the gruff side. Howard never did have much time for conversation."

"Had he had an unhappy love affair?" Marcie asked unexpectedly.

48

Ella looked at her in amazement. "Whatever could make you think that?" she demanded.

"The name of the boat. *May-Bee*. The 'May' part must be named after Peter's aunt. Maybe it was Howard who named the 'Bee' part, and it might have been after someone he knew and maybe loved."

"Well!" Ella said, almost as if this were an affront. "You *do* have some imagination, Marcie Williams! I don't think Howard Flynn ever loved anyone in his whole life, excepting himself, and I don't think anyone ever loved him, excepting maybe his own mother. No, there wasn't any 'Bee' in his life, unless every time he got near a bee it stung him because he was so ornery. 'Twas just a made-up name. May, for May Higgins, like you thought, and the 'Bee' part just to make it sound like 'Maybe.' "

"I see."

"You look disappointed. Well, I suppose it would make a nicer story if it seemed like Howard was so nasty because he was still in love with some woman who had broken his heart, but 'twasn't like that at all, I can promise you. Matter of fact, though, there was one thing he did love, besides himself."

"What?" Marcie asked innocently.

"Money!" Ella said disdainfully.

"To get back to the day of the murder," Marcie said quickly, before Ella could launch off into the matter of the late Howard Flynn's frugality, "the police know he went down to the fish pier to see about the boat, because some of the other fishermen 'saw him there?"

"That's right. Saw him and passed the time with him, talking about the weather. You'd be surprised how long fishermen can go on talking about the weather, 'specially when there's a hurricane coming up the coast. Anyhow, far as anyone knows, Howard headed straight for home after that, if you can call that miserable shack he lived in a home. At least, no one saw him after that, or if they did they're not saying. Seems likely the next person who saw him, matter of fact, was whoever killed him."

Marcie shivered. She said, "You said it happened just back of the shack, on the dunes."

"Up on top," Ella nodded. "There's a street back of the dunes that dead-ends — there's a sort of circle you can turn a car around in and some space at the side. That's where Howard Flynn always parked his truck. From there he could strike off straight across the top of the dunes; in fact, there's a sand path that leads right to those steps that come down back of his shack.

"By then, it had started to rain, and the wind was coming up. Even if we don't get the brunt of a hurricane, we get plenty of wind and the steady sort of rain that comes with that kind of a storm, just straight down, like someone had turned on a great big showerhead and pointed it toward earth.

"By then most folks were certainly in their houses — you get the urge to get snug as you can at a time like that. The only people out were those who had to be. The fishermen who saw Howard down at the pier all said that they left before he did. He must have been the last one down there. Seemed like he couldn't bear to leave the *May-Bee* for fear she might get damaged, which would cost him something."

But there had been *someone* else out, regardless of the weather, Marcie thought. She said, moistening her lips, the whole thing suddenly frightening, "How did it happen, Ella?"

"Someone sneaked up behind him in all that wind and rain and stabbed him," Ella said flatly, and despite Marcie's prodding refused flatly to say anything more.

CHAPTER 6

When Marcie awakened the next morning the sunlight was dancing across her pillowcase. She stood up to find that, although her ankle was slightly stiff, it was not so painful that she couldn't walk on it fairly easily. She went directly to the window.

She gazed out upon an especially beautiful day. The bay, she saw, was almost as blue as Peter Doane's eyes, and the sky was a slightly lighter variation of it. The sand was lemon gold; it looked as if it had been freshly washed and the shampoo had made it so much more attractive.

This was certainly the kind of day when the fishermen would be going out. In fact, Marcie suspected that Peter and his uncle had probably been up before dawn, and even now were out there somewhere beyond the visible horizon.

She wondered how long the fishing boats stayed out and when they came back to Chathamport with their catches. She knew she could ask her mother, but she also knew that if she did so Mrs. Williams might suggest that they both go to the fishing pier together.

Much as Marcie usually welcomed her mother's company, she didn't want it today! She wanted to see Peter Doane again more than anything she had wanted in a long, long while, but she also wanted to be alone when she did so.

When she went downstairs, her mother and her grandmother had already had their breakfast and were making plans for the afternoon. Marcie learned, with considerable relief, that they had asked two of her grandmother's friends over for lunch and a game of bridge.

"I don't know what that will leave you to do, Marcie," Mrs. Williams said a bit anxiously, and Marcie knew that her mother was remembering her protests about coming to the Cape for the holidays. "You probably shouldn't go walking around too much on that ankle."

"It feels much better," Marcie said quickly. "In fact, I was going to ask you if I could take the car later on. I'd like to drive around a bit and sort of get my bearings, and," she added, smiling, "I have some Christmas shopping to do!"

"Well, at least you'd be keeping off that foot while you're driving," Mrs. Williams conceded.

"There are some very attractive shops right in Chatham and many of them have sales just before Christmas," her grandmother told her. "Or, you could drive over to Orleans, if you want to. It's just a few miles, and they have all sorts of stores and shops there."

Marcie remembered her mother wondering if there would be anything open on Cape Cod at all this time of year, and Mrs. Williams thought of this, too.

"Everything used to shut up right after Labor Day," she recalled. "Now Ella tells me there are all kinds of supermarkets and condominiums and what she calls 'fancy restaurants,' and most things stay open the year around."

"Yes," Mrs. Davies nodded. "A lot of the old-timers haven't liked all the changes, but there's a good and a bad side to them. Chatham is just one of fifteen towns here on Cape Cod. Each one is quite different, and some of them made serious mistakes years ago not having tighter zoning restrictions. Now we have people like May Higgins, who's on our town Planning Board, really doing a wonderful job in trying to give us the best of two worlds. They want us to have all the comforts and conveniences of so-called civilization, while still preserving the charm of old Cape Cod."

Peter's aunt. She sounded, Marcie thought, like quite a wonderful person.

"Is May Higgins the one you were telling me about last night?" Mrs. Williams asked her mother.

"Yes," Mrs. Davies said. "They've had so much trouble."

Marcie was eager to start asking her grandmother questions about the Higginses, which would lead inevitably to questions about Peter, but she managed to restrain herself. She sensed that this wasn't the right moment to get into the story of the murder with either her mother or her grandmother. Ella was close-mouthed. It was doubtful that she would tell either of the other women about her conversation with Marcie last night, nor that Marcie had confessed she had been snooping around the late Howard Flynn's beach shack.

As for herself, Marcie decided that if she were asked directly, she would certainly tell either her mother or her grandmother about the whole incident, but right now she was not going to volunteer the information. They might very well decide that she wasn't to be trusted wandering around on her own!

She went out into the kitchen, and Ella insisted on scrambling some eggs for her to go with the sausages she had in the oven, saved from the earlier breakfast she had made for the others.

As Marcie ate, Ella said, "Well, we've finally got ourselves a beautiful day. That fog was hanging in for so long I'd begun to think 'twould never clear."

Marcie took the plunge. "Ella," she asked, "when do the fishing boats come in at Chathamport?"

Ella raised stern eyebrows. "Now, Marcie Williams — " she began.

"Mother was talking about the way we used to go over and watch them unloading," Marcie interrupted quickly. "I'm going Christmas shopping today, but I thought I might stop by at the fishing pier and watch for a while, too."

"That isn't all you'll be watching, I'd wager," Ella said tersely.

"Ella!" Marcie protested.

"Well," Ella said, "might as well tell you. You could find out most anyplace in town if I didn't tell you. The boats usually come in toward mid-afternoon, so they can get through with their work before dark."

Her grandmother had been right. There were a number of wonderful shops in Chatham. Marcie bought her mother a pair of earrings made of shells set in silver filigree, which were so lovely she nearly yielded to the temptation of buying herself a pair as well. She bought her father a tie tack made of scrimshaw, the intricate carving originally done on whale teeth by sailors long ago.

Since her grandmother was going to be confined to her wheelchair for quite a while, Marcie finally decided that it would be a good idea to give her something to do with her hands, and she knew she loved to embroider. She selected a crewel embroidery kit that would make a pillow-case bright with daisies, poppies, blue iris, and other spring flowers. It seemed to her that this would be a cheerful sort of thing to work on over the cold months of January and February, when probably many days would be as gray as yesterday.

As gray as yesterday! Yesterday inevitably made her think of Peter, and she wondered what he was doing at this very moment.

If he was as dedicated to marine biology as

Ella had indicated, he must miss college very much.

Marine biology. Marcie remembered that back in Maryland her mother had suggested she could switch her Independent Study project from the Civil War forts around Washington to marine biology! In retrospect, it seemed almost like an omen!

As she walked along the street, she paused at the window of another shop, for there was still Ella on her list — not the easiest person in the world to shop for.

Her eye was caught by something that would surely have no place in Ella's life scheme. It was a tie tack made out of pewter, in the shape of a fisherman standing at the wheel of his ship, attired in a sou'wester.

What a perfect gift it would be for Peter, she thought, if only she knew him well enough to give him a Christmas present!

The little figure seemed so familiar to her that she went into the store to ask about it, and the pleasant, gray-haired woman behind the counter told her that it was a famous replica.

"This is the Gloucester fisherman, my dear," she said, taking one of the tie tacks from a glass case and holding it out to Marcie. "The original statue is in Gloucester, right on the waterfront. The fisherman faces out to sea. The statue commemorates all the Gloucester men who have followed the sea and have been lost. There have been thousands of them. I forget the exact figure, but at one time more Gloucester fishermen had been lost at sea than the then living population of the entire town."

Marcie could not repress a shudder. Peter had spoken of the way life at sea could age a man, but she had not fully realized the dangers involved in it until now. She could only remotely imagine what it must be like to be out on the North Atlantic in a small boat in the dead of winter, surrounded by a rough and hostile ocean. Thinking about this, she felt a real pang of fear for Peter.

"Is something the matter?" the saleswoman asked gently.

"No," Marcie said quickly. "No. I . . . I'll take one of these," she said, handing back the tie tack. "Do you have a little gift box to put it in?"

"Yes, of course." The woman smiled. "Shall I wrap it for you?"

"Thank you, no. I'll wrap it myself later," Marcie told her, and knew that, once back at her grandmother's house, she would undoubtedly look at the little figure again and again before she wrapped him up.

The price of the pewter tie tack put a slight strain on her Christmas budget, and she chastised herself as she put it in her tote bag and left the shop. There was a very good chance that she wouldn't be giving it to Peter.

Well, she thought — and the thought brought a slight ache to her throat — if she didn't she would keep it forever, so that when she'd gone back home to Maryland, out of Peter Doane's life, she would always have something to remember him by!

Marcie had seen an especially pretty winter nightgown in a shop up the street, and she decided now to get this for Ella. It was the sort of thing the housekeeper would certainly never buy for herself, but Marcie was sure that she would love it, no matter how much she might protest at receiving it. It was made of soft flannel, long and full, with sleeves that ended in flouncy cuffs and another flounce edging the high-buttoned neck. The print was a pattern of small, bright strawberries entwined against a creamy ivory background.

The nightgown bought, she glanced at her watch. It was nearly one-thirty. She decided to allow herself time for a sandwich and some hot tea in the sandwich shop just across the street. She forced herself to eat slowly, because there was no point in driving over to Chathamport for at least another hour. But it was very hard to wait.

The hulls of some of the fishing boats were painted green, some blue, some red, and some were all white. They made a pretty picture as they came into port.

The men had started cleaning their catches while still at sea, and flocks of seagulls, scrounging for fish scraps thrown overboard, followed them as they chugged up the channel.

Marcie had located the fishing pier without difficulty, and she parked in a space reserved for

visitors. Walking down the hill to the pier itself
and the warehouse where the catch was received,
she had a distinct memory of coming here as a
child with her mother and Ben.

A flight of wooden steps at the right side of
the warehouse building led to the upper deck
that she had called a porch, when talking about
it to her mother.

A small Coast Guard boat, a broad orange-
and-black stripe slashing its side, was tied up at
the inner corner of the pier, almost at the bottom
of the flight of steps. Marcie wondered, as she
passed it, how often it must be necessary for the
Coast Guard to go out to rescue fishermen in
trouble. She climbed the steps, glad that she had
brought her warm parka along with her despite
the sunshine, for it was cold out in the open.

She stood at the railing watching as one boat
after another pulled up alongside the pier and
was unloaded. Marcie watched the process with
fascination, but her gaze kept straying toward
the boats farther out, still waiting their turn to be
unloaded, and her heart began to sink because
there was no one aboard any of them who looked
like Peter.

She knew that she had not been unnoticed. A
number of the fishermen had glanced in her direction, most of them smiling broadly as they did
so. Although she did not realize it, she made a
very pretty picture standing on the deck in her
jeans and bright green parka, with her coppery
hair blowing softly in the breeze.

Finally, as she was about to give up, she saw

Peter. His boat was now second in line to be unloaded, and evidently he'd been in the cabin below. An older man stood at the helm of the boat; this, Marcie thought, must be Willis Higgins, but his face was in the shadows so she could not make him out clearly.

Peter, however, as he emerged onto the deck, stepped directly into the sunlight. It seemed to turn his hair to bronze, and Marcie caught her breath as she looked at him.

At that instant, he looked upward and saw her. For a moment she was terrified. It could very well turn out that he would be angry at her for having come here. He had certainly given no indication yesterday of wanting to see her again.

To her delight, though, he smiled. He not only smiled but he waved, and she beamed back at him, waving so wildly that some of the men on the other boats grinned openly.

She watched with real interest now as Willis Higgins steered the *May-Bee* up alongside the pier with obvious expertise, and the unloading began. There had been two men to handle this task on most of the boats and normally there would have been two men on the *May-Bee*, but Willis Higgins's back must still be giving him trouble, Marcie concluded, for Peter did all the heavy work himself.

With the fish unloaded, Willis Higgins stepped up onto the pier and was lost to sight somewhere in the recesses below. It was Peter who took the helm now, maneuvering the boat toward a mooring near a small island just offshore, which was literally covered with waiting seagulls. He took a pail, tied it to the end of a long rope, and dipped it over the side of the boat, hauling it back and sloshing down the boat deck. He repeated this performance several times as Marcie watched him. Then, briefly, he went below, reappeared to step into a small dinghy that had been tied to the mooring, and began to row toward shore.

Marcie didn't want to be totally obvious. She waited until two more boats had unloaded their catches, and then she went back down the steps, hoping that Peter might be waiting for her.

She didn't see him at the bottom, and slowly she started back to the car, her footsteps lagging. Her ankle was beginning to hurt, and she knew that she had walked around on it too much in the course of her morning's shopping.

She was limping by the time she was halfway up the hill to the parking area, and she was talking to herself at a fierce rate, telling herself that she really had been a fool.

Despite his smile and wave, Peter Doane clearly hadn't wanted to see her. She had just about thrown herself in his face, she thought, her cheeks burning with the humiliation of it, and she could imagine what Ella would say if she found out about it.

"Might think you'd know a mite better!" She could almost hear Ella's flatly accented voice, clipping out an opinion that could only be considered the right one.

"Marcie!" She heard her name called and

turned to see Peter running up the hill toward her.

He had taken off his yellow foul-weather gear, and he was wearing a heavy wool, blue plaid jacket, left open to reveal a light tan, wool shirt. His deep blue eyes were sparkling with what seemed to be genuine pleasure.

"It was so great to look up and see you standing there!"

"Well," she said, "I'd been out doing some Christmas shopping, and I remembered how Mother used to take my brother and me over to see the fishing boats come in when we were here visiting Grandmother Davies years ago."

As she spoke, she was extremely conscious of the little pewter fisherman nestled way at the bottom of her tote bag, back at the car.

"I'm glad you decided to repeat history," Peter told her. "Yesterday I . . . well, I really couldn't come in when you asked me to. But I . . ."

"Yes," she prompted.

The smile faded from his face, and he bit his lip. Marcie, watching him, was in an agony of apprehension. But then he smiled again, although it was a rather wistful smile, and he said, "Well, I *did* hope we'd run into each other, somehow. That is, I was hoping we'd see each other again."

That was all Marcie wanted to hear.

CHAPTER 7

As they were standing together, Marcie heard the sound of an approaching motor, and a pickup truck drew up alongside them and slowed down. A heavyset man with a weatherbeaten face and grizzly gray hair was at the wheel. Although she had not been able to get a clear view of his face while he was aboard his boat, Marcie realized that this must be Willis Higgins.

Once, she thought, he might have been handsome. Now life, or the sea, had taken its toll. Willis Higgins doubtless looked much older than he actually was and his face was haggard. Even if she hadn't known about Howard Flynn's murder and the resulting cloud that hung over Peter's uncle, this man would somehow have seemed tragic to her.

Higgins leaned out the truck window, ignoring Marcie and speaking directly to Peter.

"Coming along?" he asked.

"Not just now," Peter said, to Marcie's relief. "I've got a couple of errands up in town."

Higgins nodded without further comment and drove off.

Peter, watching the truck turn left onto Route 28, said slowly, "That was my uncle."

"I imagined so," Marcie admitted.

He looked at her so directly that there was no chance of evading that blazing blue gaze.

"By now," he said, not without bitterness, "I imagine you've gotten most of the story out of Ella Mayo."

Marcie flushed, which was a giveaway. "You make it sound like Ella is a real gossip!"

"No," Peter said soberly, "she isn't. But I realize she's known you most of your life and I imagine you have quite a way about you when you want to."

"What do you mean by that?" she asked him defiantly.

He smiled wryly. "I had something of a taste of your 'way' yesterday, Marcie," he reminded her.

"Peter . . ." she began.

"Yes?"

"Peter . . . I'll admit I did ask Ella about you."

"Yes?"

"She thinks a lot of you."

He was watching her quizzically but he said only, "Well, I'm glad to hear that. I think a lot of both Ella and your grandmother."

His face sobered, and — just as he had yesterday, when they were walking up the beach and he spoke of the harshness of life at sea — he suddenly looked tired and older.

"Marcie, it doesn't really matter. Unless you stayed right there in your grandmother's house all the time you were here, there's no way you wouldn't have heard about the situation with my uncle and me. It's as well you heard the story from Ella. At least I'm sure she told you the truth. That's more than I can say about a lot of the tales being spread around town lately."

"What are people saying?"

"Some of them are insinuating that my uncle and I were both in on a plot to kill Howard Flynn. They figure we ganged up on him together."

"But that's *terrible!*" Marcie protested.

"Yes, it is," he agreed quietly. "It's one reason why I didn't stop in at your house yesterday when you asked me to. It would be better if you weren't involved with me right now."

Marcie could not repress a laugh, and he looked at her, surprised.

"Ella put it a different way," she told him.

"How did Ella put it?"

"Well, I can't quote her exact words, but she said something about your having enough on your plate without adding me to it," Marcie admitted.

"That sounds like Ella. She's right. I do have enough on my plate. But that has absolutely nothing to do with you," Peter said firmly.

"I'm glad to hear you say so."

"Hey," he protested, "I didn't mean what that may sound like. What I'm saying is that I don't agree with Ella's interpretation, but the facts do still stand, Marcie. Right now it would be better if you weren't seen with me."

66

"That's ridiculous!" Marcie told him. "I'm sure my grandmother and Ella would both agree with me about that, that there's no reason why I shouldn't be seen with you. Unless, as Ella seems to think, I'd just be a nuisance to you."

At moments there seemed to be a shadow over Peter's face, the same sort of tragic look that Marcie had noted on Willis Higgins's stern countenance. Now the shadow lifted, and his smile was warm.

"I can't imagine you'd ever be a nuisance to me, so we won't say any more about it, okay?"

"Okay," she agreed, her heart suddenly much lighter.

They began to walk the rest of the way up to the parking lot, side by side, and Peter said, "You're limping. You've been overdoing it on that ankle by going Christmas shopping."

"Now you sound like Ella."

"Well, when you get home you should soak your foot in hot water for a while, and then take a rest until dinner time," he told her.

"Yes, doctor," she mocked him. They had come to the visitors' parking lot and she said, "Where's your car?"

"I don't have one," he admitted.

She frowned. "You told your uncle you were going to do some errands up in town, didn't you?"

"Yes."

"Well, how were you going to get there?"

Peter grinned, and held up his thumb.

Marcie forced herself to look very stern. "I don't usually pick up hitchhikers," she told him.

"I certainly hope not!" he said firmly.

"However, in this case" — she couldn't repress her laughter any longer and she waved to the car — "get on in."

"How about letting me do the driving so you can prop up that foot and give it some rest?" he suggested.

For her answer, she handed him the car keys.

As he got in, he glanced into the backseat and saw her tote bag full of packages. "Wow!" he said. "You really *have* been doing your Christmas shopping, haven't you?"

"There are so many neat shops," she told him. "I could have kept right on going, to tell you the truth. I saw a lot more things I would like to have bought for people. My funds are getting on the low side, though."

He laughed. "My funds are on the low side all the time, lately." Again, that shadow seemed to fall over his face. "Anyhow," he confessed, "I never seem to be able to get up much enthusiasm about Christmas."

Marcie remembered Ella's telling her about the terrible accident in which his parents had been killed, and he had been injured. It had been just before Christmas when he was twelve.

She could feel that clear blue gaze sweep her face and she flushed; it was almost as if he could read her thoughts.

He said, "Ella covered a lot of ground, didn't she?"

She was so embarrassed she wished she could shrink until she temporarily became invisible. She said, "Peter . . . I . . . well, I don't know what to say. I admit I *did* get Ella to talking about you, but please don't hold it against her. Blame it on my curiosity, if you must blame it on anything."

"I'm flattered that you should be curious about me," he said drily, but when she looked at him his face was as blank as Ella's was sometimes.

"You're not flattered," she contradicted him flatly. "You think I'm nosey, and I don't blame you."

To her surprise, he said, "Well, you *were* nosey, weren't you?"

She hesitated, hating this. Then she said dismally, "Yes, I was."

Surprising her again, he laughed. He said, "I like an honest answer, and so I'll give you one in return. I *am* flattered that you were curious about me, Marcie, and that's the truth. It's just that I . . ."

"Yes?"

"Well," he said, and he kept his eyes straight ahead, on the road, as he said it, "the whole business about Christmas and my parents is something I just don't talk about."

"I can understand that. I'm not asking you to talk to me about it, if you don't want to," Marcie told him. "But I'm sure you know without my telling you that it doesn't do a person any good to keep something like that bottled up inside, year after year after year."

His smile was slight, but it *was* a smile. "Playing shrink?" he accused her.

"No. I'm not qualified."

"That doesn't stop most people! Marcie, I'm older than you are —"

"Only four years," she told him. "I'm seventeen."

"Whew! Ella really *did* fill you in, didn't she," he teased her. Then he went on, his voice quiet now, "I was going to say that you would remember what it is like to be twelve even better than I do. At that age, you're sort of on the threshold between being a child and beginning to grow up. You're just beginning to find yourself — you have a lot of confusing, conflicting feelings."

It wasn't that hard to think back, Marcie found. "Yes," she said, "that's so."

"Twelve's an age when a kid really needs security, a kind of base he can rely on," Peter told her. "Oh, any age would be a hard one at which to lose your parents, but I think twelve is an especially rough time. I was twelve that November, and the next month my parents and I were on our way up here to spend Christmas with Aunt May and Uncle Will when it happened. It had been snowing, it was slick driving on the Jersey turnpike, there was a big oil truck . . . and it skidded. All I remember was that one minute we were singing Christmas carols, my mother and I — and my father was telling us we were off-key — and the next minute this giant shape just loomed up in front of us."

Tears filled Marcie's eyes. She wanted to touch

him; she wanted to do something to alleviate the pain in his voice. She reached out and put her hand on top of his, and he glanced at her, his blue eyes seeming darker than usual.

"Let me get through with it," he said, his voice thick. "Would you believe I've never said this much about it to anybody before, not even to Aunt May? There were just the three of us, my mother, my father, and I. I was sitting in the back seat. We had two or three shopping bags filled with Christmas presents, like the packages back there in your tote bag, except these were all wrapped up. I guess when the crash came the presents slid all over me — all I can remember is sort of a whirl of red and green and after that everything went black.

"I just dimly remember the terrible noise of the crash, and my mother screaming and my father calling out her name. Her name was Helen. As I've said, after that everything went black . . . which was merciful. I never saw my parents again."

"Oh, Peter," Marcie whispered.

"I was in the hospital by the time I became fully conscious; there were sort of fuzzy periods in between that I don't really remember, but when things got clear Aunt May was sitting there by my bed. She couldn't bring herself to tell me about my parents. She went and got Uncle Will, and I don't think anyone in the world could have handled it more beautifully than he did.

"After a while, though, when it really began to sink in, I heard them singing Christmas carols,

Jeanie read page 73
after you read page 71. They
got 72 and 73 mixed up.

beneath her chin, and he gently forced her to look up at him.

"Are you thinking of becoming a psychiatrist, by any chance?" he asked her.

"No," she stammered. "No, I'm not."

"You just might make a good one," he told her, and before she could speak again he bent down and very lightly brushed her lips with his.

"Before we continue this analysis, Dr. Williams," he said then, to her astonishment, "how about coming in and letting me buy you a cup of coffee?"

Tim's Place was obviously a favorite rendezvous with the fishermen. Men with rugged, weatherbeaten faces crowded the counter that ran along one side of the small combination restaurant–variety store. Everyone seemed to know each other, and there was a steady hum of conversation and laughter.

There were a few booths at the back of the restaurant section, and Peter led her to one of them, exchanging greetings with a number of the men as he passed them. He also paused to speak briefly to the stocky, gray-haired man with steel-rimmed glasses who stood behind the counter pouring out coffee as quickly as he could, with the help of a slim, pale, blond girl.

"That's Tim Bailey," Peter told Marcie, as they settled into a booth, nodding toward the gray-haired man. "The girl helping him is his daughter Trudy. They always have their hands full after the boats get in, but it's even worse in bad

72

off somewhere in the hospital. It was years before I could even *listen* to a Christmas carol without feeling that I was going to throw up.

"Anyway," he said, taking a deep breath first, "that's the way it was, Marcie. When I was twelve years old I knew there would never really be another Christmas for me."

They had driven past Chatham Center, and now Peter was pulling into the parking lot at a small shopping complex. Midway along the group of stores Marcie saw a sign, TIM'S PLACE, ornamented with a cup of coffee etched in gold-toned neon light that glowed through the deepening afternoon.

Peter parked, that closed look on his face again, and he said, "So now you know about it."

"Yes," she said, "but you're wrong!"

His eyebrows shot upwards, in surprise. "What do you mean?"

"Your parents would never have wanted you to spend the rest of your life shutting out Christmas," she told him bluntly. "That's a terrible thing to do to their memory. I can understand how you feel, but don't you think it's time you *did* grow up a little, and let some of your sorrow wash away? Christmas is supposed to be a time for peace and love among people, not a time to keep on reliving tragedy, no matter how terrible!"

When she had finished speaking Marcie was aghast at herself, and briefly wished that she could shrink into invisibility. She was afraid to look at Peter; then suddenly she felt his finger

73

weather when the fishermen can't go out at all. Then everyone hangs out here, except when they're looking for beer instead of coffee. Then you'll find most of the fishermen in the Buoy Bar, up closer to the center of town."

Watching the men, Marcie said, "It must be fun to live in a place where you know everyone."

"Sometimes it is, sometimes it isn't," Peter said. "When things are going well, it's fine. When there's trouble, though, you could use a little more anonymity!"

He was thinking, Marcie realized, of his uncle and their inevitable involvement with Howard Flynn's murder. Flynn, before his death, must have been one of the regulars at Tim's Place, she imagined. Or had he been? Everything she had heard thus far indicated that Flynn had been a loner, keeping pretty much to himself. Probably, after the day's work was done, he headed back to the beach shack and made his own coffee.

Thinking about this reminded her of the coffee pot still on the grimy stove in the shack, covered with that thick scum of green mold, and she shuddered.

"Cold?" Peter asked. "Look, I'll go get us some coffee. Trudy really does have her hands full. Would you like a doughnut or something to go with it?"

"No, thanks," Marcie said. "Ella's feeding me so much I'm afraid I'm not going to be able to get into the dress I bought to wear on Christmas!"

As she watched Peter go up to the counter and

talk with Trudy Bailey, Marcie couldn't fail to notice how the girl's cheeks became flushed with color, and there was a look in her eyes as she spoke to Peter that caused Marcie to frown.

You didn't have to have a crystal ball, she told herself, to see that Trudy was — what was that word Ella used? — smitten with Peter. The astonishing thing was that he seemed so totally oblivious of it. His smile was friendly, nothing more.

He really doesn't have any idea of how attractive he is, Marcie thought, as he brought back coffee for both of them, and a large cinnamon bun for himself.

He said, putting her brimming cup in front of her, "I ordered yours regular — is that all right?"

"What's regular?" she asked him.

"New England for 'with both cream and sugar,'" he grinned.

"That's fine," she told him, and took a sip. The coffee was really good, and she said so.

Peter nodded. "That's one reason why Tim's Place is so popular. The fishermen come for coffee — sometimes I think they have more coffee than blood in their veins. They can always be sure of getting *good* coffee here at Tim's, and his baked stuff is always homemade, too. He has two or three local women who bake for him, since his wife died a couple of years ago."

"Doesn't his daughter go to school or anything?"

"No," Peter said, "not at the moment. Trudy is my age; we went to high school together."

"Oh?" Marcie asked, a bit coldly. "She looks younger."

"Yes, I suppose she does. She has a lovely voice. She used to sing at concerts when we were in school. The fall after we got out of Chatham High I went to URI — that's the University of Rhode Island — and Trudy went to Boston, to the New England Conservatory of Music. She was doing well — Aunt May says they thought Trudy might have a real future in music. Then her mother died and Tim needed her to come back and help him run this place."

So, Marcie thought, both Trudy Bailey and Peter had been forced to abandon their studies to come to the aid of relatives.

It gave them a common bond she didn't particularly relish!

CHAPTER 8

As they drank their coffee and Peter munched on his cinnamon bun, Marcie was conscious of the fact that Trudy Bailey was glancing over in their direction every time she had an opportunity to do so.

Peter was telling her about the fishermen coming in and out, and about some of the town characters, lacing his accounts with humorous anecdotes. They had finished their coffee and were about to leave when Trudy walked across to them.

"More coffee, Peter?" she asked, her light gray eyes fixed upon his face.

"Thanks, no, Trudy," he told her. "Marcie, this is Trudy Bailey. Marcie is Mrs. Davies's granddaughter, Trudy. She and her mother have come up to spend Christmas."

Trudy's smile seemed friendly enough; possibly, Marcie thought with an irony that was unlike her, it was because the other girl realized that she was only a temporary visitor.

"That's nice for Mrs. Davies," she said. "Ella Mayo takes good care of her, I know, but it would still be lonely at Christmas without some of her own family around."

Trudy turned to Peter. "I meant to tell you," she said now, "they're having a carol program at church Christmas Eve, and I'm to be a soloist. I hope you'll come, Peter, and it would be nice if you would come with him, Marcie."

Marcie sensed so acutely that Peter was about to refuse that she intercepted before he could speak.

"I would love that," she said, and in this she was sincere.

Peter gave her a brief look that was so cold she literally felt chilled by it, and she glanced quickly at Trudy. The other girl had, however, turned to answer something her father had asked her and had missed Peter's obvious displeasure.

He said stiffly, "I'll be glad to bring Marcie, Trudy," and Marcie realized that the words were hard for him, and that she should have talked to him before she accepted so quickly. He glanced at her, and again it was as if he were reading her mind. He swallowed rather hard and said, warmly enough, "I'd really like to hear you sing again, Trudy. It's been a long time."

"Yes, it has," Trudy said. Her smile was rueful. "It's been quite a long time since I've done any real solo work. I've been singing in the church choir regularly, and once in a while I do have a small solo, of course. But this will be different."

Peter nodded and didn't pursue it, but when he and Marcie were outside again he said, as

78

they were walking to the car, "You deliberately got me into that one, didn't you!"

She didn't try to pretend that she didn't know what he was talking about. "Yes, I did," she said frankly.

"I suppose this is your idea of therapy or something?"

"I suppose it is," she admitted, looking rather woebegone.

He surprised her again. "I suppose you may be right," he said grudgingly. He looked down at her, his blue eyes very intent. "Whatever all of this may do to my feelings about the holidays," he told her, "I'm sure that this is going to be one Christmas I'll never forget!"

The bridge party was just breaking up when Marcie got back to her grandmother's house. She was introduced to her grandmother's friends and then, in the flurry of departures, she managed to get up the back stairs with her Christmas presents, and to hide them in her bedroom closet.

For dinner, Ella fried tiny bay scallops until they became crisp morsels of golden goodness, and she had made fresh cole slaw and home-fried potatoes. With Indian pudding for dessert, topped with a dab of vanilla ice cream, Marcie was so full that she was more than ready to settle in by the fireplace and play cribbage with her grandmother, until she got so sleepy she excused herself and went to bed.

It was beautiful again the next day, but Marcie really had overdone it, as far as her ankle was concerned, with her Christmas shopping. She awoke to find it really sore and swollen. This time her grandmother, her mother, and Ella all insisted that she stay in and keep her foot up, and she was powerless against all three of them.

She propped herself up against some pillows on her bed and spent a good part of the day writing Christmas cards, most of them with long messages describing the Cape, her grandmother's house, and Ella. Only to Jayne Minton, her best friend at Ashburton High, did she confess that she had met someone who was truly terrific!

As she wrote her messages, Marcie's attention wandered periodically. She kept watching the clock on her bedside table, knowing, as it got close to three, that Peter and his uncle would be coming in about now to unload their catch at the pier.

She tried to tell herself that maybe her sore ankle was a sort of omen; she couldn't very well show up at the pier every afternoon as the fishing boats were coming in. Despite the fact that Peter obviously had been glad to see her and despite the memory of that light kiss sweeping across her lips, it would be embarrassing to him if she were to haunt his place of work. And she'd never been one to chase after boys, not even when it was a boy whom she felt strongly about.

With this thought it came to her that she never *had* felt about a boy the way she felt about Peter. She had never been much of a believer in the old cliché about love at first sight, nor was she now. Still, something had sparked between Peter and her, almost from that first moment in the shack when he'd been so terribly angry at her.

She sensed deep within her this was a spark that could flame into something real and true and long-lasting. She also realized that at this point, it was a fragile thing, which could so easily be extinguished — especially on Peter's side. As Ella had said, Peter had a lot on his plate right now. He had told her he couldn't imagine her ever becoming a nuisance, but was this entirely so? Right now he really didn't need a serious involvement with a girl.

A serious involvement! Marcie shook her head, chiding herself for jumping to conclusions. If she kept on going this way, she stood a good chance of being hurt! She reminded herself that she and Peter had been together only twice. Their first encounter had hardly been under ideal circumstances, and she had precipitated the second one.

Like it or not, the next move was up to Peter!

She went downstairs for dinner, trying not to hobble, because she knew that tomorrow she absolutely must get out of the house and do something. She hoped that in the course of that something she would meet Peter.

There were only two more days till Christmas Eve. Would Peter get in touch with her about Trudy Bailey's concert? It would be easy enough for him to let it slip by, especially because he really didn't want to go.

Despite her best efforts she did limp, and Ella said, "Another hot soaking for you after dinner,

Miss, and then I'm going to redo that elastic bandage." Ella had insisted upon taking on a doctoring job earlier in the day, mumbling as she did so that she should have gotten out the elastic bandage for Marcie's ankle in the first place.

Now she said, "I can tell just looking at it that it's too loose. It's got to be tight, but not too tight."

Marcie groaned inwardly, but she knew that the housekeeper was right.

Tonight Ella would not even think of letting her help with the dishes. Once again she played cribbage with her grandmother, but she warned Mrs. Davies that tomorrow they were going to tackle backgammon, which was very popular right now.

Her grandmother laughed. "It's a very *old* game," she told Marcie. "It was a very old game when *I* learned how to play it, and I was younger then than you are now."

"All right, then I'll take you on," Marcie said firmly. "I brought a set with me because Dad and I often have a game or two before dinner."

As she spoke, she could hear the telephone ringing in the little back parlor her grandmother used as a library and study. There was an extension in the kitchen, and it was usually Ella who answered the phone, as she did now, coming to the parlor door to say to Marcie, "It's for you."

"For me?" Marcie was honestly startled.

"It's Peter Doane," Ella said succinctly, and Marcie caught the flash of surprise in her grandmother's eyes.

She took the phone in the study, because she couldn't stand the thought of having Ella's eyes upon her as she talked.

She heard the click of the receiver in the kitchen as she said "Hello," and she smiled. Whatever you might say about Ella, she wasn't an eavesdropper!

"Marcie?" Peter asked.

"Yes."

"I met Ella Mayo up at the post office this afternoon," Peter said. "She was mailing a batch of Christmas cards for you. She said you couldn't mail them yourself because your ankle was acting up."

Ella, the witch, had never said a word! Marcie said, "I could have driven up with them, Peter. It's just that my ankle was swollen this morning, and my mother and my grandmother and Ella have kind of been martinets about it."

"Well, they should be," Peter said firmly. "I should have been more of a martinet yesterday. I should have driven you straight home instead of taking you to Tim's Place."

"I hardly did any walking at all at Tim's Place," she pointed out.

"Well, you did plenty when you were shopping, and then later, walking up and down the hill at the fish pier," he said. "Marcie . . ."

"Yes?"

"Ella says she's about to make you soak your foot again, and then she's going to bandage it up and put you to bed."

83

"I've been *on* the bed most of the day," Marcie said. "And I'm not particularly sleepy."

"Nevertheless, Ella's right this time around," Peter said. "I was going to suggest we find a movie you haven't seen, but why don't you do as Ella says tonight. Maybe you'll be ready to go out tomorrow night, okay?"

Marcie could feel her pulse thudding. "Okay!" she said, so glad he wasn't going to scoop her off that plate of his that she wasn't about to argue!

When Marcie returned to the parlor her grandmother was still sitting near the fireplace, her wheelchair rolled up to the card table with the cribbage board set up on it.

Mrs. Davies looked at her granddaughter closely, and Marcie wished fervently that she could escape the question almost certain to follow.

"I couldn't help but overhear Peter Doane's name," Mrs. Davies said, mildly enough. "When did you meet him, Marcie?"

"When I was walking on the beach, the first afternoon I was here," Marcie said, which was certainly the truth — as far as it went.

Mrs. Davies said thoughtfully, "I've known Peter ever since he came here to live with May and Willis Higgins after his parents were killed. I've always thought he was a very fine young man, and that it was a pity he needed to drop out of college this fall."

Marcie, anxious though she was to speak, managed to remain silent as her grandmother

84

went on. "As I imagine you may already know —
you seem to have gotten around a bit, Marcie,
the short time you've been here — there has been
a lot of trouble in the Higgins family."

"Yes," Marcie admitted, "I do know. I think it's
unfair it should reflect on Peter, though."

"Possibly it is," Mrs. Davies admitted, "but
small towns still are small towns, Marcie. This
supposed age of wonders we're living in hasn't
changed people all that much. When there is a
violent death in a town like Chatham, you can't
begin to imagine the echoes it sets off."

"I think," Marcie ventured timidly, "that perhaps I can. But I still don't feel it's fair for anyone to blame Peter for what has happened."

"Do you know that there were hurricane warnings up the day Howard Flynn was murdered?"
Mrs. Davies asked unexpectedly.

"Yes, as a matter of fact I do," Marcie said.

"You don't know what that meant, however,"
her grandmother continued. "You've never lived
by the sea; you can't possibly appreciate the effect it has on one's life, Marcie, even those of us
not directly connected with earning our living
from it. When there are hurricane warnings
posted, everyone gets busy battening down their
own hatches."

"I suppose they must," Marcie agreed.

"To put it more directly," Mrs. Davies went
on, "when a storm of major proportions is head-
ing our way, we tend to become immersed in our
own affairs to a considerably greater extent than
we might be at other times. People were still

85

preparing for what might have been the direct attack of a hurricane, when Howard Flynn was killed. As it was, we had quite a blow, lost our power, and many among us were kept busy for a period of time worrying about protecting our own property. If it hadn't been for that, the murder might long since have been solved. It's hard to hide things in a small town. If it hadn't been for the storm, there might have been witnesses to the murder, clues. As it is, it has been difficult, if not impossible, for Chief Bearse and his men to prove anything, don't you see?"

Marcie looked across at her grandmother, and her lovely hazel eyes were troubled. "Are you trying to tell me that you think Willis Higgins killed his partner, and if there hadn't been a storm, it would have been proved at the time?" she asked.

"No, darling. What I'm trying to tell you is that, except for the storm, I think we'd know by now whether or not Will Higgins *is* guilty. I can't believe, myself, that he possibly could be, despite the evidence against him. So I might add that, if it hadn't been for the storm, we might know by now who *did* kill Howard Flynn."

"What about Peter?" The words were little more than a whisper.

"Personally," Mrs. Davies said, "I don't think Peter was even *in* Chatham at the time Howard Flynn was killed. I think he deliberately camouflaged his own movements in order to try to give his uncle an alibi, and in so doing he has only succeeded in casting suspicion on himself, as well as on Will Higgins."

Mrs. Davies sighed. "It is a very complicated matter, Marcie, and I don't pretend to judge. I am only telling you that there are ugly rumors about both Peter and his uncle, and there will be until the murder is solved."

"I had coffee at a place just outside town yesterday with Peter," Marcie said. "There were a lot of fishermen in there, and they all seemed friendly enough to him."

"I daresay his uncle wasn't along?" Mrs. Davies suggested.

"No, he wasn't."

"That's just it. Will has virtually gone into hiding since this happened. He's a sensitive man under the gruff exterior he presents to the world. But many people think his attitude is as good as an admission of guilt. Then they go on to argue that Peter is young enough, brash enough, to try to bluff it out."

"That's ridiculous!" Marcie said hotly. "There is nothing brash about Peter, and I don't think he could bluff anything out if he tried."

"Then stick to your own convictions, Marcie," her grandmother told her, unexpectedly. "Just be prepared, if you go out with Peter, to see some eyes cast in your direction that may not be entirely friendly, or even to hear people whispering some ugly things."

"I couldn't care less!" Marcie said defiantly.

"I'm glad you feel that way, dear," her grandmother said. "Too many of us are quick to con-

87

demn before the facts are in. At this point, neither Peter Doane nor his uncle honestly know which of the people here in Chatham are their friends, and which are their enemies. I think Peter needs a friend, and I'm glad that you've chosen to stick by him."

Before Marcie could recover from her surprise at this statement, her grandmother added softly, "Now, if you're going to go out tomorrow night, you'd really better get off that ankle."

CHAPTER 9

They had decided to go to the first show, since Peter had to get up very early in the morning to go fishing with his uncle.

"There's a chance we won't be going out, though," he told Marcie, as they waited in line at the ticket window of the movie theater. "The weather seems to be taking a turn for the worse, and it could snow tomorrow."

"The day before Christmas Eve," Marcie said, forgetting Peter's feelings about Christmas. "Oh, that would be wonderful! Do you think maybe we really will have a white Christmas? Grandmother says they're pretty rare, here on Cape Cod."

"That's true," Peter said easily enough, and Marcie nearly sighed audibly, she was so relieved. The last thing in the world she wanted to do was to make him uptight about Christmas, or anything else.

They were into the theater, now, and it was nearly time for the movie to begin. The lights dimmed, and they watched the picture; but later Marcie didn't remember what it had been about.

It was, they agreed as they left the theater, an average movie at best; but Marcie had the feeling that even if it had been an Academy Award-winner it could not have held her attention tonight. Her thoughts were entirely on the boy at her side. There was so much she wanted to know about him, so much she wanted to ask him.

They drove past the shopping center where Tim's Place was, and she noticed that the lights were out.

Peter, following her gaze, said, "Tim caters pretty much to the fishermen. He opens very early and he also closes early. I thought we'd go on over to a place in Harwich — that's the next town up the Cape — and get some coffee. If you'd like to, that is."

"I'd love to," she said quickly.

Most of the shops were staying open late these last couple of days before Christmas, so many of the people in the coffee shop had shopping bags full of packages.

Marcie stole a glance at Peter. What a constant reminder of the terrible tragedy in his life the Christmas season must bring him each year.

They found a vacant booth for two, and ordered coffee and apple muffins. As the waitress left them, Peter smiled across at Marcie and said teasingly, "Think you'll still be able to get into that dress you plan to wear Christmas Day?"

It seemed to Marcie as if a small victory had been won. He could say "Christmas," and he could smile when he said it.

She laughed. "I may have to use a couple of

safety pins," she told him. And then, suddenly, a marvelous idea struck her. "Peter," she said, the words coming out before she could stop to think about what she was saying, "would you and your aunt and uncle come and have Christmas dinner with us? It'll be just my father and mother and Grandmother Davies and me. My brother Ben is with the Navy in the Mediterranean and we're going to miss him so terribly. It would be so great to have someone about his age with us and —"

Her words stopped as suddenly as they had begun when she saw the way he was looking at her. He was smiling, but it was a sad smile, and there was something about the expression in his eyes that made her want to cry.

"Marcie," he said gently, "your heart is too big for you."

She stared at him dumbly. "I'm not sure what you mean by that."

"Have you asked either your grandmother or your mother about this?"

"No," she admitted. "But I know they'd love to have all of you and, if you want me to, I'll go to the phone over there in the corner and call them right now!"

She started to wriggle out of the booth, but he laid a restraining hand on her arm, and his touch, the warmth of his palm, sent a sensation coursing through her that she had never felt before.

"Marcie," he said, "hold it!" Then he said, more gently, "I'll never forget your asking us, Marcie . . . and I only wish I could accept your invitation. I know Aunt May would love to accept it, and you'd like each other. But neither of us can get Uncle Will out of the house these days. He goes straight to the boat and straight home again, and that's the way it's been ever since the police took him in for questioning after they found Flynn. I don't think he'll ever get over the shame of being suspected of murder . . . unless the real killer is found."

"It must be terrible for your aunt," Marcie said.

"Yes, it *is* terrible for her."

"And for you, too," she persisted.

He hesitated, then he said, "Yes, it has been pretty rough for me, too, there's no use denying it."

Marcie took the plunge. "Where were you when Howard Flynn was murdered, Peter?" she asked him.

For a moment she thought he wasn't going to answer her. Then he said, "I was on my way back from Falmouth. That's up at the upper end of the Cape, near the Cape Cod Canal."

"You mean," she said, "you were *miles* away from here?"

"A good forty miles, I'd say," Peter admitted grimly. "I was majoring in marine biology at URI, and last summer I was able to get a job at Woods Hole Oceanographic Institute, just outside Falmouth."

She stared at him. "If the police know about this," she said, "how can they possibly suspect you of anything?"

"I'm not sure they do," he told her. "They've

never come out and made any flat accusations against me, just against my uncle. Chief Bearse even wanted my uncle to take a lie detector test, but Tom Chardwell — he's my uncle's attorney — Tom Chardwell advised against it."

"Why?"

"I gather those tests aren't always foolproof," Peter said. "I don't know. I wish he *had* taken it. I think it would have made him look better. But it wasn't up to me to make the decision."

Thoughts could not help but flicker through Marcie's mind. Had the attorney been right in prohibiting Willis Higgins from taking the lie detector test? Was Peter blindly loyal to his uncle? It was understandable enough if that were so, but was there a chance that Willis Higgins *had* killed his partner?

She said, frowning, "Peter, did you tell the police where you were at the time of the murder?"

"No," he said flatly.

"But why not?"

Peter sighed deeply. He toyed with the spoon on his saucer, and when he looked across at her his eyes were miserable.

"I owe an awful lot to Aunt May and Uncle Will," he said simply. "They're all the family I have. There was no one else to take me in after my parents were killed. If they hadn't been willing to, I would probably have become a ward of the state and spent my growing-up years in an institution.

"As it is, they welcomed me, they made their home my home. Even though I know Aunt May

93

always wanted children and couldn't have them, it certainly couldn't have been easy to take a twelve-year-old boy into a household where there had never been any kids before. Especially a twelve-year-old boy who had such a long way to go to get over the physical injuries he'd gotten in that accident — and was pretty messed up emotionally as well."

"You certainly don't show any effects of the accident now," Marcie said.

"*Physical* effects, you mean?" he asked her. "Well, I have one nasty scar on my right thigh that doesn't do much for me when I'm wearing bathing trunks, and another on top of my head, but my hair grew back, so that one's camouflaged. The psychological scars, as you've already noticed yourself, are something else again. Emotional things take longer to heal, Marcie."

"I can see that," she admitted. "I can also see why you feel so indebted to your aunt and uncle. But I can't see why you should have put yourself in the position of being a possible murder suspect."

His smile was wry. "I don't know what it is about you, Marcie, that brings out all these confidences," he told her. "What I'm telling you, I might add, is *strictly* confidential."

"I realize that!"

"Okay, then. You've heard all about the hurricane warnings that were up the day of the murder, haven't you?"

Marcie nodded.

"Well, as it happens, Uncle Will had strained

94

his back. His doctor told him to stay home and lie flat as much as possible, or he could be in for some real trouble, even an operation.

"Surgery was the last thing he needed. He was having a hard enough time of it just keeping the *May-Bee* going. You've heard that old saw about the bark on a tree being tight? Well, Howard Flynn was a lot tighter! After Uncle Will went into partnership with him and they pooled everything they had and bought the *May-Bee*, Uncle Will soon realized that Flynn's whole idea of a boat was to get as much out of the sea with it as he could, and put back as little as possible into its upkeep.

"Unfortunately," Peter added, "that's not an unusual viewpoint among commercial fishermen. They take their hard-earned money and put it everywhere except back into the boats they depend on not only for their their living, but for their very lives. This is one of the reasons why there are so many sea tragedies, why boats go down each year, especially during storms.

"Anyway, Uncle Will has always kept up on things. He wanted to equip the *May-Bee* with some of the new, sophisticated types of sonar and radar gear that would have made her much more effective when it came to locating fish, and also a lot safer. With the right kind of equipment you don't have to wait till you get a storm warning on your marine radio to know what's coming up!

"At the very least, Uncle Will wanted to put the boat in drydock from time to time for some

95

really necessary repairs to the engines and the hull, and Flynn flatly refused to go along with any of this."

"Well, what about your uncle?" Marcie asked. "If they were partners, didn't he have as much to say about the boat as Flynn?"

"No," Peter said ruefully, "unfortunately he didn't. When they went into the *May-Bee* together, Flynn, who was an old bachelor and had evidently hung on to every cent he ever made, put more cash into the venture then Uncle Will did. He owned fifty-five percent of the *May-Bee*, Uncle Will owned forty-five percent. Uncle Will is so honest it never occurred to him there could be trouble because of this. He thought he and Flynn were in business together, with one mutual aim. It was quite a while before his eyes really began to open where Flynn was concerned.

"Toward the end, the two of them were quarreling more and more, because the *May-Bee* was getting in worse and worse shape. Right now we shouldn't be using her, to tell you the truth. She should be taken out of the water for the rest of this winter and thoroughly overhauled. She's still a good boat, but she needs an awful lot of work."

"But your uncle persists in using her as she is?" Marcie asked, appalled.

"It isn't a matter of choice, Marcie," Peter said bluntly. "It's a matter of paying bills. Just the lawyer's fees are really something."

"But that's so wrong!" Marcie pondered for a moment, and then she asked, "Who owns Flynn's share of the *May-Bee* now?"

"No one, at the moment," Peter said. "What would be his share of the profits go directly to the bank here in Chatham that's acting as his executor. His estate is all tied up; his lawyers are looking for a distant cousin who would be his heir. Supposedly this cousin moved to California years ago, and so far they haven't been able to find him. In the meantime, the court has given Uncle Will permission to keep on operating the *May-Bee* because it *does* represent his livelihood."

"You said," Marcie began slowly, "that your uncle and his partner had been quarreling quite a bit, before the murder?"

"Yes," Peter nodded. "That's what has made it particularly difficult. People around town, people who used to see the two of them in Tim's Place, as well as the fishermen down at the pier, all know they weren't getting along, and that their disagreements were getting worse. That hasn't helped."

"But to get back to you — you'd been at Woods Hole all summer? You hadn't been working with your uncle on the boat?"

"That's right. When I got the chance to work at Woods Hole, both Aunt May and Uncle Will would hear of nothing else. That was back in June, right after the semester ended in college, and even though their personal relations were pretty strained, Uncle Will and Flynn were still working together without too much difficulty. Flynn always was a loner anyway — he never had much to say to anyone — and Uncle Will is a quiet sort of person. It was easier for them than it might have been for two more outgoing people to simply take the boat out and fish, bring in their catch, and then go their separate ways once the day's work was over.

"Also, at that point, Uncle Will hadn't hurt his back. He did that in early August, when he was trying to do some work on the boat that no man should have attempted singlehandedly. He tried to keep right on working, which he admits now was idiotic of him — it really cinched it with his back. Actually, he shouldn't be working now. He has to wear a back brace, and he's in pain quite a lot of the time."

"This all must be very hard on your aunt," Marcie said.

"She loves him," Peter said simply. "They went to school together, here in Chatham. Aunt May went away to teachers' college; she has more formal education then Uncle Will, but he has a kind of basic common sense and intelligence, I guess you might say. He has a head full of lore about the sea, and everything concerning it, that you could never get from books. It was he who got me started toward marine biology, and Aunt May, who teaches science at Chatham High, took it from there.

"Anyway, Uncle Will went right to work after high school. He'd fished all those years, but for most of them it was as a hand on somebody else's boat. His dream was to own his own boat, but it costs a lot of money to buy a fishing boat of any account. When Aunt May came back from college, he sort of had the idea for a while that she was too good for him. I think it was she who changed that notion and they got married. They're about the most devoted couple I've ever seen."

"My mother and father are like that," Marcie told him.

"Then you and I are both lucky to have grown up around such people," Peter said. "Today marriage is a joke a lot of the time." The blue eyes were direct. "When I get married," Peter said, "I want it to be forever."

"So do I," Marcie told him, her voice barely rising above a whisper.

She couldn't help but realize, though, that even if he was looking at *her* he just might be thinking of Trudy Bailey. There was a parallel to the story of Trudy Bailey and Peter, and his aunt and uncle. He and Trudy had gone through school together, too, and their fortunes had brought them both back to Chatham. The only difference was that in their case neither of them had been able to finish their education.

This was an area Marcie really didn't care to dwell on, so she said, "You still haven't told me what really happened with you the day of the murder."

"Well, they were as concerned at Woods Hole about the idea of a hurricane hitting as they were every place else on the Cape," Peter said. "I got to thinking about Uncle Will and that bad back of his, and how his first thought was going to be for the *May-Bee*. He was always the one to go down to take care of things like that. Howard Flynn, ordinarily, couldn't have worried less — he knew Uncle Will would do everything and he let him do it. Ask any fisherman and he'll tell you that Flynn sat out most of the storm warnings at a table all by himself in the corner of the Buoy Bar!

"Anyway," Peter continued, "I called Aunt May and she admitted that she was having a hard time keeping Uncle Will down. She said that Howard Flynn *had* stopped by — he never did have a phone in that beach shack of his — and said he'd go down and look after the boat. She admitted that Uncle Will didn't really trust him to do the job, and she said they couldn't afford any damage to the *May-Bee*. There was enough work to be done on her already without adding to it.

"I told Aunt May I'd try to get away as soon as I could and head home. Well, the hurricane never did hit us straight on, but we got all the side effects; it was a very close call. I started out from Woods Hole, and by then the winds were terrific and the rain was coming down so heavily there were times when you couldn't see to drive. I thought it would be best to go across and hit the Mid-Cape Highway. It runs right down the center of the Cape."

"I know," Marcie nodded. "Mother and I took it the other day on our way here."

"Well, in this case it was a mistake. That day, it was so bad, between the wind and the rain, that I had to pull off at the different rest areas along the way. So it took me longer to get home than it would have normally. I never did bother to clock the time; I was so intent just on getting back that it didn't occur to me to keep glancing at my watch.

"When I finally got home, my aunt was fixing some supper on a Coleman stove we have — it uses bottled gas — because the power had gone out by then. My uncle was lying on the couch in the living room, resting.

"The wind wailed all through that night, and we continued to have a downpour. Nobody was even thinking about Howard Flynn then, or until it cleared the following afternoon. Then they started checking around to assess the storm damage, and that's when Flynn's body was found, lying on the path that crosses the dunes to those steps back of his beach shack."

"But your uncle had an alibi, if he was forced to keep off his feet because of his back, and if your aunt was right there with him," Marcie protested.

"It would seem so," Peter conceded. "But she *is* his wife, and I've always had the feeling Chief Bearse didn't believe the story she told him." Peter hesitated. "Also," he admitted then, "I've got to admit that I wonder about it myself. Ever since this happened, Marcie, my aunt hasn't been herself. She's been losing weight, she's tense, she jumps when you walk into a room unless she hears you coming first."

"That seems natural enough, when your husband's living under the kind of cloud your uncle has been living under," Marcie pointed out.

"I suppose so," Peter said reluctantly. "But . . . I think it's more than that, Marcie. I think Aunt May knows something that has her worried half to death, and no matter how much I've tried I can't get it out of her."

CHAPTER 10

Peter had been right. The next day, the day before Christmas Eve, it did begin to snow, but it melted almost as soon as it touched the ground.

It made everything seem cold and wet and gray; it was not the sort of snow, Marcie thought, gazing out her bedroom window, that promised to provide a white Christmas.

She was restless; although her ankle was better, it really wasn't good enough for beach walking, and she knew Ella would be quick to point that out if she suggested going out of doors.

She spent part of the morning wrapping up her Christmas gifts, including the little pewter fisherman. She wrapped the box that contained him in especially pretty paper, blue sprinkled with silver stars, and put a silver-and-white bow on top. She remembered Peter's telling her that his next-to-last memories of the accident had been a red-and-green whirl of colors as his family's Christmas presents cascaded across him. Instinctively she chose these other colors when wrapping his gift. She was not at all sure of how she was going to get his gift to him, but she'd figure out a way.

As she wrapped his present, she went over the night before. She had asked him about his having dropped out of college.

He had said, sadly, that he could see no other way. The scholarship he had been given would have made him financially independent, but his uncle really needed his help. With his bad back, it would have been impossible for Willis Higgins to fish the *May-Bee* alone, and he was too proud a man to settle back and accept unemployment compensation and live on his wife's earnings as a teacher.

"So, instead, he was willing to sacrifice you. Is that it?" Marcie asked bitterly.

"He didn't want me to drop out, Marcie," Peter said levelly. "Also, I'm sure you can imagine how it upset Aunt May. But I felt it was what I had to do. I'm young enough to go back to school when all this clears up, and some day it *has* to clear up, or I don't know what will happen to both Uncle Will and Aunt May. But until Flynn's murder is solved my place is here with Uncle Will. He took me in and helped me when I needed it."

There was a tone to Peter's voice that made it clear he was not about to change his mind in this respect, no matter what she might say to him, and Marcie had decided, dismally, that she had no right to be saying as much as she had. Although she felt she knew this handsome, wonderful boy almost better than she had ever known anyone, she had to admit that she had known

104

him only for a very short time. In many ways they were still strangers.

Peter had used his uncle's car to take her to the movie, an old blue Ford that was getting rusty on the sides. The climate on the Cape; he told her, pointing to the rust spots, was hard on car finishes, due to the salt air.

When he had left her at her grandmother's door it was not much past ten, and she thought of asking him in but then decided against it. She knew, somehow, that he would refuse.

She had almost said something about the Christmas Eve concert at which Trudy Bailey would be singing, and for which they had a date; at least, she hoped he considered it a date. Something also kept her from mentioning this, and Peter had said nothing about it.

Thinking back, she realized that she might very well not hear from him at all about the concert, feeling as he did about Christmas, and especially Christmas carols. He could simply avoid the whole thing by not getting in touch with her.

Unfortunately, too, she could almost believe after last night's end that he very well might not want to get in touch with her at all again. He had been silent and almost stern when they pulled up at her grandmother's house. Once again he had looked considerably older than his twenty-one years, and there had been an expression of weariness on his face that almost translated into defeat.

She had hoped he might kiss her good night,

but he didn't. He only nodded when she thanked him for the movie and the coffee and let her slip out of the car by herself.

At lunch she was so quiet that her grandmother looked across at her quizzically and said, "You've something on your mind, Marcie, and it doesn't seem to be settling very well with you. Why don't you share it with your mother and me?"

"Well," Marcie said reluctantly, "it's about Peter Doane."

"I suspected it might be," her grandmother said, a faint gleam of amusement in her dark eyes.

"Grandmother, I did something I really had no right to do last night," Marcie admitted.

"Oh?"

"I suggested to Peter that he and his aunt and uncle have Christmas dinner with us."

"Marcie," her mother protested, "you *didn't* have any right to offer an invitation like that. This is your grandmother's home, remember?"

"Yes," Marcie said almost angrily, before her grandmother could speak. "I *do* know that, but you don't have to worry. Peter refused the invitation anyway."

"Did he really?" her grandmother said softly, and now there was a speculative look in her wise, dark eyes. "Did he refuse you before he had even consulted his aunt and uncle?"

"Oh," Marcie said impatiently, "he said his aunt would love to come — he was sure of that — but his uncle doesn't go anywhere anymore."

106

"From everything I hear," Mrs. Davies said, "That does seem to be so."

"But it's so wrong, Grandmother," Marcie protested. "Any one of a number of people could have killed Howard Flynn."

"Oh?"

"Yes! No one in town seems to have liked him, from what I've heard."

"I don't know just what you've heard, Marcie," Mrs. Davies said mildly. "I'm not about to say that many people liked Howard Flynn, either, from what *I've* heard. But do you realize the sort of weapon he was killed with?"

Marcie frowned. "I know he was stabbed."

"Yes, stabbed in the back. The murderer left the knife right in place. It was a fisherman's knife, Marcie."

Marcie paled slightly, but after a moment she rallied and said, "I saw any number of fishermen in Tim's Place the other afternoon, Grandmother. Most of them looked pretty strong; I guess they have to be to do the work they do. From what I understand, none of them liked Howard Flynn, so why couldn't it have been one of them who killed him?"

"It might very well have been," Mrs. Davies conceded. "The police have found no real motive, however, that leads to any of the other fishermen. That's the problem, you see. Willis Higgins had good reason to become angry enough to kill his partner, and everyone — including the police — knows it."

"Don't you think that makes it pretty obvious?" Marcie demanded.

"Obvious?"

"Grandmother, Willis Higgins is such an *obvious* suspect, it seems to me the police ought to realize that if he'd been the one to commit the murder he would have been more clever about it. As it is, if he did kill Howard Flynn it's almost as if he went to a lot of trouble to point suspicion right at himself."

"Yes, it may seem that way," Mrs. Davies agreed, "but much as I love mystery novels, Marcie, murder in real life is sometimes quite a simple affair. Someone comes to the end of his particular rope and acts. In this case, I think that Will Higgins was coming to the end of his rope with Howard Flynn, nor — from what I've heard around town — can he be blamed for that. But no one has the right to take another life, Marcie."

Marcie was staring at her grandmother. She said, "You think he did it, don't you?"

"Marcie, darling, I hope more than I can possibly tell you that Will Higgins didn't kill his partner. I just don't know, that's all."

With that, Marcie had to be content.

That night after dinner Ella came to the door of the living room, and it took only a glance to know that something was seriously wrong. Her gaunt face was ashen.

She looked directly at Marcie, and Marcie's heart contracted. Even before Ella spoke, she knew that something had happened to Peter!

"Marcie," Ella said, without preamble, momentarily ignoring both Mrs. Davies and Mrs. Williams. "Clara Eldridge called, just now. She's an old friend, and she lives next door to May and Will Higgins. She says this afternoon someone sneaked up on Peter Doane just like they did on Howard Flynn, last August!"

CHAPTER 11

Marcie sprang to her feet, ignoring the pain that shot through her ankle. Her mother was at her side in an instant, and even her grandmother tried to get up but was thwarted by the heavy cast on her leg.

Ella was wringing the corner of her apron with her long, bony fingers, and she said quickly, "'Twasn't with a knife, Marcie. Good heavens, I didn't mean to scare you half to death. Peter is alive."

The relief was so overwhelming that it made Marcie giddy. She staggered slightly, and her mother put a warm and comforting arm around her shoulders. "Was he hurt badly, Ella?" Mrs. Williams asked.

"I don't know," Ella admitted. "He's still at the hospital. They're taking X-rays."

"Did Clara say what happened?" Mrs. Davies put in.

"Peter was on his way to that blasted beach shack, that much seems certain," Ella said. "He had a lantern with him, and he was walking across the path atop the dunes. It's foggy out;

you know the way fog seems to cover the sound of footsteps, muffles just about everything, matter of fact. Someone sneaked across behind Peter and hit him over the head.

Mrs. Davies was tight-lipped. "Who found him?"

"Some folks — think their name is Lopes — they only moved here a couple of years back. They live in the old Crowell house at the end of the street right back of the dunes," Ella said. "They happened to look out their side window and thought they saw flames. Did, too. It was a kerosene lantern Peter had, and it spilled out over the beach grass and set fire to it. It had started to snow again, so the fire didn't get very far.

"It's lucky it started at all," Mrs. Davies said. "If it wasn't for that, he might still be lying there."

Marcie shuddered. "Grandmother," she implored, "can you talk to Mrs. Higgins? Can you find out how he is?"

"Yes, Marcie, I can," her grandmother said firmly. "Constance, wheel me into the library will you? I'll use the phone in there."

As Marcie followed, Mrs. Williams wheeled her mother across the wide-boarded floors of the old Cape Cod house and up to the desk where the phone was. Marcie noticed that her grandmother's hand was trembling slightly as she dialed the Higgins's number, and there was real concern in those fine, dark eyes.

She likes Peter and his family even more than

111

she has admitted, Marcie thought suddenly, and despite her own worry she felt especially tender toward her grandmother.

There was no answer that first time they called, and this was almost too much. Marcie began to cry, and as her mother turned toward her she said, "I'm going to drive over to the hospital my-self!"

"Wait until I can get some word," her grand-mother cautioned her.

But although she tried again and again over the next twenty minutes, there was no answer. Finally, when Mrs. Davies was about to agree to Marcie's driving to Cape Cod Hospital, if her mother would go with her, she dialed one more time and May Higgins answered her phone.

Mrs. Davies stated very briefly that they heard Peter had been injured, and May Higgins took the conversation from there. As Marcie watched in an agony of frustration, her grandmother nodded at her encouragingly and finally said, "Wait just a minute, will you, May?"

She held her hand over the phone receiver and turned toward her granddaughter.

"Peter's all right," she said. "A bad bump on the head, plus a slight cut, but nothing more. They released him after the X-rays had been checked, and he's home now."

"I want to see for myself," Marcie insisted stubbornly.

Mrs. Davies spoke into the telephone again. "May," she said, a hint of humor in her tone, "my granddaugther seems to have become quite a friend of your nephew's in the short time they've known each other. Would it be too much of an inconvenience if she and her mother stopped by your house in a little while, for just a few minutes?"

May and Will Higgins lived in a gray-shingled cottage on a lane that branched off Chatham's Main Street. There were lights shining in the front windows as Marcie and her mother pulled up. The door was opened to them before they even had a chance to ring the bell.

The woman who stood in the doorway was about Marcie's mother's age, although now she looked so tired and so worried that she seemed older. There was a faint resemblance to Peter in her features, and her eyes, while not so blue as his, somehow had the same expression about them. Under better circumstances, Marcie thought, May Higgins would be a very pretty woman.

She welcomed them cordially and led them into a typical Cape Cod parlor, for this, too, was an old house, with low-ceilings and wide floorboards.

Marcie's eyes, however, were only for Peter, who lay on a couch that was barely long enough for him, a thick bandage wound around his head.

As soon as he saw her he tried to get to his feet, and it was her mother who waved him back.

"Stay right where you are, Peter," Mrs. Williams admonished. "I'm Marcie's mother, I'm afraid it would have been impossible to keep her away from here tonight, after she heard about your accident."

"It wasn't an accident." A voice spoke behind them and they turned to see Willis Higgins standing in a doorway that evidently led into a small dining room. He looked older and more haggard than he had the day Marcie saw him at the fish pier. "Someone deliberately attacked the boy," he said, "and I only wish I could lay my hands on him!"

"Will," his wife warned, but he shook his head.

"I've had more than I can take when things like this begin to happen," he said heavily. "The next thing we know, whoever killed Howard Flynn will be after you, May!"

There was something about the way he made that statement, a despair, perhaps, that finalized Marcie's own feelings. She was convinced now, that no matter what anyone might say, Willis Higgins had not killed his partner. She was equally convinced that the true murderer must be uncovered. Until this happened, neither Peter nor his aunt, nor his uncle would really be safe. At the moment she could not think further into the implications of this, for Peter was looking across the room at her. Their eyes met and locked.

May Higgins noted this silent communion between her nephew and this lovely, copper-haired girl and she said, almost briskly, "I'm going to fix us all some mulled cider. There's nothing like a hot drink on a night like this. Why don't you and Will come out into the kitchen with me, Mrs.

Williams, so that Marcie and Peter can talk together?"

As the older people left the room, Marcie looked after May Higgins gratefully. She pulled up a hassock close to the couch where Peter lay and sat down.

"That was nice of your aunt," she told him.

"My aunt is a very nice person," he said with a faint smile. "So are you, to come over here like this, Marcie."

"I *had* to come," she said simply.

He reached out a hand, and she entwined her fingers in his. He asked, "How did you know about it?"

"A friend of Ella's called her up," Marcie told him. "Peter, what were you doing?"

"We tried to go out this morning," he told her, "but we had to put back. The weather was simply too bad. My uncle wouldn't have tried it in the first place, but this whole mess has been costing him much more than it should. He's been paying a retainer fee to the lawyer, and if you ask me Chardwell is fleecing him. I've never liked him, especially since he also did some legal work for Howard Flynn."

"Why did your uncle pick him?"

Peter shrugged. "I suppose because he drew up the partnership between Uncle Will and Flynn in the first place, so Uncle Will felt he knew him. I think it was a bad choice, though. I don't feel that Chardwell has done nearly as much for Uncle Will as he might have."

115

"So you decided to take matters in your own hands?" she chided him

"I keep feeling there must be something in Flynn's shack in the way of a clue," Peter admitted. "I was going to see if I could find anything the day I met you, and this is the first chance I've had to get back there since."

"You might have asked me to go with you," Marcie pointed out.

"Ask *you*? You're out of your mind, Marcie," he told her, clearly horrified at the thought. "This isn't fun and games, you know."

"Yes," she said, almost angrily, "I *do* know. Peter, do you have any idea who hit you?"

He started to shake his head but winced, and she asked quickly, "Does it hurt very much?"

"At the moment, yes. The cut isn't so much, but they took four or five stitches so I guess I can add another scar to the ones I already have. I have to go back in the morning for a checkup, and I imagine they'll remove the turban effect then. They were a little bit afraid this might have stirred up my old head injury.

"I guess I have a thick skull, though," he added. "No fractures or anything like that."

"Oh, I'm so glad," she whispered.

"I haven't forgotten," he said suddenly, "that we're going to hear Trudy sing tomorrow night."

She looked up at him, her eyes glistening with tears. "I doubt you're going to be up to anything like that," she said unsteadily.

"Look, the doctors promised me a fair headache tonight, and maybe on into the morning,

116

but I don't intend to keep it forever," he said, trying to laugh. Then he added, softly, "You're about to cry, and I don't have a handkerchief handy. I don't want you to cry over me, anyway."

She brushed away the tears with her sweater sleeve, and she tried to laugh. "Okay," she told him, "I'll try to be a spartan New England type. But Peter, I was so frightened. When Ella came to the door and said you'd been attacked, just like Howard Flynn —"

"That's what she said?"

"Yes. I don't think she realized the conclusion that I would leap to, and I don't even want to think about that."

His grip tightened. "Marcie —" he began.

"It's okay," she interrupted. "I'm not going to dissolve into tears on your shoulder, honestly I'm not. It's just that . . . well, if anything terrible had happened to you I think I would have felt much worse about Christmas for the rest of my life than you do."

As he had once before, he tipped her chin so she had to gaze directly into his deep blue eyes, and she caught her breath at the expression she saw in them.

"Marcie," he said, "I think you should know I've begun to feel different about Christmas now that I have you to share this one with."

Before she could answer him, Mrs. Higgins came in with a tray holding two mugs of steaming mulled cider.

Marcie standing, said, "We can put the tray

right on this hassock if you like, Mrs. Higgins, and I can sit on the floor."

May Higgins smiled. "That's fine, if you think you'll be comfortable, Marcie. I understand you twisted your ankle the other day."

"Yes, but it's much better." Marcie curled up on the floor next to the couch as if to emphasize this point, and Mrs. Higgins laughed as she put the tray down on top of the hassock.

When she had left the room, Peter said, "That's the first time I've seen my aunt smile like that, let alone laugh, for a long while. You're a wonder maker, Marcie."

"I wish I were," she said wistfully. "I wish I could really do something for your aunt and uncle."

"You have," Peter said. "Coming here tonight as you have, and your mother coming, too, means a lot to them, I know. I'm not saying that everyone around town has abandoned them since this happened, because that isn't so. There are those who have stuck by them, as well as those who have turned their backs. That's one thing about an experience like this. It very quickly proves who your real friends are."

They slowly sipped the cider, which was spiced with cloves and cinnamon and maple syrup and was really delicious, but then, glancing at Peter, Marcie saw that he had closed his eyes. She said quickly, "Your head is really hurting, isn't it? I think it's time I called mother and we went home, so you can get some rest."

He opened his eyes, and managed a smile. "Do you suppose it might be possible for you to kiss me good night first?" he asked her.

It was entirely possible.

CHAPTER 12

Although the skies were gray on Christmas Eve morning and snow threatened again, no flights had been canceled, and Mrs. Williams and Marcie set out to meet Marcie's father at the Hyannis airport.

As she drove, Mrs. Williams said, "I can understand why you've come to like Peter Doane so much. He's a very attractive young man."

"He's extremely good-looking, I know, Mother," Marcie admitted, "but he's so much more than that. He has . . . well, I guess you could call it real character."

Mrs. Williams nodded. "That's the impression I got from both his aunt and his uncle," she agreed.

Marcie was surprised. "Did Mr. Higgins actually talk much to you?" she asked.

"Both Mr. and Mrs. Higgins talked to me considerably more than I expected they would," Mrs. Williams admitted. "I think the attack on Peter was such a terrible shock to them they had to let some of it out," she went on. "Also, they have sensed Peter's confidence in you, Marcie. So I think they felt that they could trust me."

Marcie said dully, "Someone really hates Peter and his uncle."

"I think someone is very much afraid of both Peter and his uncle," Mrs. Williams said. "Whoever killed Mr. Higgins's partner may believe that Peter or his uncle or both of them have some real evidence against him."

"If they did, they'd take it to the police," Marcie protested quickly.

"Yes, I'm sure you're right about that. However, the murderer may not be quite rational in his thinking, Marcie."

"You mean he's insane?"

"No," Mrs. Williams said. "What I mean is that he's been living with the knowledge of his own guilt all these weeks and watching others suffer for the crime he committed, namely, Peter and his uncle. It seems to me that would be enough to unhinge almost anyone, and make them suspect things that are not necessarily true. The murderer may think that Peter or his uncle have some definite clues to his identity, but for reasons of their own have not gone to the police with them."

Mrs. Williams went on, soberly, "I tried to tell Mr. and Mrs. Higgins that they should report yesterday's attack on Peter, but Mr. Higgins was very stubborn about it. He has come to detest Chief Bearse, which is too bad. My mother says that actually the Chief's a decent man, trying to do his job, and has nothing personal against either

121

Will Higgins or Peter. Mr. Higgins, though, has lost faith in the entire Chatham police department. It must be very difficult to face the fact that people who have been your friends suspect you of murder, when you know that you are innocent."

"Then," Marcie said, her sense of relief overwhelming, "you believe that Peter and his uncle are innocent. Don't you, Mother?"

"Yes," Mrs. Williams said firmly. "Yes, I do."

They were nearly at the entrance to the airport when she added, "I invited the Higginses to Christmas dinner with us, Marcie, and they accepted."

Marcie's eyes spoke volumes, telling her mother all the things she wanted to say and couldn't find words for.

Mr. Williams was used to traveling all around the world, and had always stressed the importance of traveling light. Usually, he said, he could get everything he might possibly need in the course of an entire trip in a single suitcase. Both his wife and daughter were surprised, therefore, to see him reclaim two large suitcases when he went to get his baggage after the plane had landed. Laughingly he admitted, as they walked across the parking lot toward their car, that one was full of Christmas gifts.

On the drive back to her grandmother's, her father said, "Awfully quiet, aren't you, Marcie?"

"Marcie had a rather upsetting experience last night," her mother answered quickly. "A friend of hers was injured, and we were afraid for a while it was worse than it turned out to be. I'll fill you in later, Fred. Now, tell me about everyone in Bethesda."

Marcie, huddled in the rear seat of the car, smiled at the back of her mother's head. It was no wonder, she thought with an inward smile, that her mother was so successful as the wife of a Foreign Service officer. There were moments when she was, indeed, the very soul of diplomacy!

"Marcie, Peter Doane called while you were gone," Ella told her as she walked into the house.

"How is he?" Marcie asked quickly.

"He's as bad as your grandmother. He insists he's fine. He says the carol concert is at seven tonight, and he'll pick you up at six-thirty, if that's okay. He was afraid it would put our dinner hour off, but I told him we could eat early."

Mr. Williams was raising his eyebrows. "Is this the injured friend?" he asked.

"Yes, it is, Daddy," Marcie admitted.

"Peter Doane is one of the finest young men in Chatham," Mrs. Davies said, her voice as definite as Ella's had been. "I've an idea. Why don't you bring him back after the concert, and we'll wait to trim the tree till then."

"Grandmother," Marcie said hesitantly, "I don't know whether Peter would want to do that or not."

"Why wouldn't he?" Mrs. Davies asked, surprised.

"Well . . . Peter's parents were killed in a car

accident just before Christmas, when he was only twelve," Marcie said slowly. "Christmas has very tragic memories for him, and he tries to avoid everything about it as much as possible."

"Yet he's taking you to a carol concert?" her father asked quizzically.

"Yes, but he was more or less trapped into that," Marcie admitted.

"I doubt Peter would let himself be trapped into something he didn't want to do," Mrs. Davies said. "He doesn't seem the type to me. I think this is a new beginning for Peter, Marcie. I'd bet he'll come back with you tonight."

"We'll see," Marcie said, but she was doubtful about it.

During the afternoon, Marcie kept thinking about Trudy Bailey, wondering if anyone would remember to send her some flowers to wear for tonight's concert.

Even though she suspected that Trudy might be in love with Peter — and this was not a thought that appealed to her in the slightest — there had been a wistfulness about the pale, blond girl, a sadness, that was unforgettable.

On an impulse, Marcie borrowed the car and drove into town, went to a florist, and selected a corsage made of tiny red-and-white rosebuds tied with a green bow. She had already decided that if Tim's Place was closed she would find out where the Baileys lived and take the flowers right to Trudy's door.

To her relief, there were still lights on at Tim's

124

Place but, as she walked up to the door, Marcie saw Tim Bailey himself locking it from the other side.

She tapped urgently on the glass pane. He glanced up, his steel-rimmed glasses catching the light so that she couldn't really see his eyes, and shook his head negatively, pointing to the "Closed" sign he had placed in the window.

Marcie shook her head back, just as definitely, and held up the box she was holding. She tried to silently mouth the words, "For Trudy," so that he might understand her.

Finally he shook his head in bewilderment and reluctantly unlocked the door. Obviously, he was not pleased.

"What do you want?" he demanded, his tone almost surly.

"I wanted to see your daughter, Mr. Bailey," Marcie told him.

He seemed surprised that she knew his name, but he said only, "Trudy's out back finishing up, then she's got to get home. She's singing at church tonight."

"I know," Marcie said. "I'm going to hear her." She gestured toward the box. "I have something for her," she said, and added staunchly, "and I'd like to give it to her myself."

Tim Bailey looked annoyed rather than pleased, but he stepped back and called, "Trudy," in a loud voice, and a moment later the blond girl appeared in a back doorway.

It seemed to Marcie that she was thinner and paler than ever, and dark shadows of fatigue underlined her eyes. Certainly she didn't look at all as a girl should who was going to be the star of a concert that very evening!

"Oh," she said, when she saw Marcie, and Marcie stepped forward hastily.

"I'm Marcie Williams," she said, "I was in here with Peter Doane the other day and he introduced us. You may not remember —"

"Oh, I remember," Trudy said. She looked puzzled. "We're closing," she said. "Did you want something?"

"Just to see you for a minute, if I may," Marcie said. "I . . . I have something for you."

As she said this, she suddenly felt shy, wondering if Trudy might not think it downright ridiculous of her to have bought the flowers. They didn't even know each other, after all. Would this frail girl — who looked much more tired than she had any right to look — take the gift in the spirit in which it had been intended, or would she get the impression that Marcie was merely sorry for her?

Trudy glanced at her father and said, "Why don't you go ahead, Dad? Perhaps Marcie would drop me off, after we've talked a minute. It's right on your way back to your grandmother's, Marcie."

"I'd be glad to," Marcie agreed eagerly.

"I'll lock up, Dad," Trudy told her father, but the big, gray-haired man only mumbled something dourly. He almost glared at her as he went out of the coffee shop, closing the door behind him.

Trudy locked the door as soon as he had left, then turned out the front lights.

"This way, no one will bother us," she told Marcie. "I . . . I hope you won't mind Dad. He hasn't been himself ever since Mother died, Marcie. She was sick for so long first; that took a lot out of him, but it's been even worse since she died, and that's nearly two years now. He just can't seem to shake it."

"It must make it pretty hard for you," Marcie said sympathetically.

"Well . . ." Trudy smiled faintly. "If I didn't have my singing, even just singing with the choir at church, I don't know what I'd do," she admitted. "Look, we've emptied the coffee urn out but I can make us a cup of tea, or some instant."

"No, thanks, I've got to get back home," Marcie said. She held out the box. "Peter and I are coming to the concert tonight," she said, "and I thought it was so nice of you to include me in your invitation I wanted you to have these."

Trudy looked almost shocked. Slowly she took the box, putting it on the counter, and Marcie said hastily, "Open it."

"Now?"

"Yes. It's for tonight, Trudy. If you want to wear them, that is —"

She broke off as she saw the expression on Trudy's face when she glimpsed the flowers. The girl's pale blue eyes filled with tears, and she said shakily, "These are so lovely they'll make me feel like a queen. I'm wearing a white dress. It's the same one I wore at our senior concert in high school. I'm just hoping that's long enough ago so no one will recognize it. These will help camouflage it."

She hugged Marcie briefly.

"I'm so glad you're coming," she said, and added, an odd catch in her voice, "I won't forget your doing this, Marcie. In fact, I'll never forget you."

CHAPTER 13

There was certainly nothing forced about
Peter's smile when he came to pick Marcie up
that evening, and his blue eyes were anything
but sad.

She met him at the door, ready to leave.
She had already decided that the time to intro-
duce him to her father would be when they returned to trim the tree, even though she still
held her breath slightly at the thought of extend-
ing this invitation to him.

Marcie was not one to put things off, though.
She had learned early in life that if something
had to be faced it was best to face it and get it
over with!

Thus, once he had settled her by his side in his
uncle's battered old car and they were driving
toward Main Street and the big, white, typically
New England church where the Christmas program was to be held, she got to the point.

"Peter," she said, "we usually trim our tree
Christmas Eve afternoon, but this year we decided to wait till later, so you could help us."

She was almost afraid to look at him. Finally,

as the silence between them lengthened, she stole a glance in his direction, and saw, her heart sinking, that he was staring straight ahead, his expression unreadable.

"Peter . . ." she began again, tentatively, prepared to tell him that she would understand if he didn't feel he could come.

But to her surprise he turned and smiled at her, and there was a tenderness to his smile that brought a catch to her throat.

"Dearest Marcie," he said gently, "I'd love to come and trim your tree with you."

The church was beautiful; lights were streaming out the stained glass windows so that the night seemed ablaze with jewels. A huge holly wreath, with the most enormous red satin bow Marcie had ever seen, decorated the front door, and the altar had been banked with freshly cut greens interspersed with red and white poinsettias.

Soon the strains of "The First Noel," "Hark the Herald Angels Sing," and the other lovely and familiar carols filled the church.

Then Trudy stepped to the center, right in front of the altar. In her long white gown, with Marcie's flowers pinned on her shoulder and her blond hair brushed till it shone, she looked almost like an angel herself.

She started to sing, and her voice was angelic; her soprano tones soared as she sang the "Gloria." When she finished, the audience could not refrain from wild applause. She bowed as gracefully as any opera artist and obliged by singing "Silent Night" for them. When she had finished there was hardly a dry eye in the church.

Later, there was a small reception in the church hall downstairs, and everyone clustered around Trudy, congratulating her.

Marcie noted Tim Bailey standing aside, by himself, sipping a cup of cranberry punch. His face was set in its usual stern lines and, Marcie thought, it was impossible to tell whether or not he was pleased by his daughter's obvious success.

Peter pointed out one of the men crowding around Trudy was Tom Chardwell, his uncle's attorney. He was a big, red-faced man with a shock of white hair, a nose that could only be described as bulbous, and a booming laugh that, to Marcie's ears, had a false note about it. He looked like a heavy drinker, and Marcie couldn't help but wish that he was not Willis Higgins's lawyer. Even though her mother had cautioned her again and again about the fallacy of making snap judgments about people, there was something about this man she neither liked nor trusted.

When Trudy saw Marcie and Peter she managed to break away from her admirers and came toward them, her eyes glowing.

"Oh, Trudy," Marcie told her, her own eyes shining, "it was so beautiful!"

"Thanks to you, Marcie," Trudy said. "You may not realize it, but it was you who really gave me the courage to do it when you came over to the shop this afternoon."

She reached up on tiptoe and whispered something in Peter's ears, and he looked surprised. But it was not until they were leaving the church that he said, "Trudy told me you sent her those flowers. It was . . . well, it was the nicest thing you could have done. If I weren't such a clod I might have thought of it myself. Trudy's never had much of that kind of attention, not here in Chatham, anyway."

"Her voice is so beautiful," Marcie said. "She should be back at the conservatory."

"Yes, she should be," Peter agreed grimly.

It had begun to snow again, but this was a different kind of snow, thick white flakes that drifted down to cover the Christmas tinsel and holly wreaths, coating fences and tree boughs with a very special kind of frosting.

There were Christmas candles with bright blue bulbs in each window of her grandmother's house, and they glowed softly in the night. Peter held her arm as they went up the front walk together, saying, "Watch it with that ankle of yours. It may still be a bit weak, and this is kind of slippery here."

"I love the snow," she said, as they paused in front of the door and she fumbled for her key. She laughed up at him, snowflakes catching in the sheer wool scarf she'd put over her hair when they came out of church.

Peter seemed about to say something, but instead he clasped her very gently as he bent his head down, and his lips found hers. Her arms stole up around his neck and as they kissed they clung together for a moment that, in itself, seemed lost in time.

It was Peter who released her. He said, a bit unsteadily, "Hey, we'd better get inside."

Peter and her father took to each other immediately, Marcie saw with relief. She was sure her mother had told her father by now all about the murder, Willis and May Higgins, and Peter himself. Constance and Fred Williams, their daughter suspected, kept few secrets from each other, which was one reason why theirs had been a singularly happy marriage. There was certainly nothing in her father's attitude, though, to indicate that the story had upset him, and for this Marcie was grateful.

When later all the ornaments had been put on the tree, Peter and Marcie carefully added tinsel icicles, one at a time.

As everyone put their presents beneath the tree, Marcie was very conscious of the small, blue-wrapped package that she had hidden on a bookshelf in the back parlor. She wanted so much to give Peter his present now, but she wanted to be alone with him when he opened it.

Finally it was Peter who had said, "Marcie, do you suppose I could talk to you alone, for just a minute?"

Marcie, suddenly feeling very shy in front of him, nodded, and led the way into the back parlor. As she went across to the bookcase, to get

Peter's gift, she wondered what he might think about her having bought him a present. Then, when she turned around, she saw that he had a small package in his own hand, and he had chosen the traditional red and green colors in which to wrap it, as if to emphasize the fact that he had managed to put the past where it belonged.

He seemed as surprised to see her package as she was to see his, and after a moment in which neither of them said anything they both burst out laughing.

Then Marcie said, "Peter, we never do open our presents till Christmas morning, but I want to open your gift now!"

"I want to open your gift now, too," he assured her.

There was a special excitement to this moment as their fingers fumbled with the wrappings, and then they were each opening small boxes, and each exclaiming at the same time.

He had given her a shimmering silver seagull, fashioned with its wings outspread as if it were in flight, suspended from a slender silver chain.

"I thought," he said unsteadily, watching her as she exclaimed over it, "that it might always remind you of Cape Cod, and this Christmas and . . . hopefully . . . of me."

"It always will," she said, her own voice trembling. "Peter . . . put it on for me, will you?"

He carefully fastened it around her neck, and then held out the tie tack. "How about you putting this on for me?" he suggested.

As she pinned the little fisherman onto Peter's dark blue tie she voiced her own kind of silent prayer. May you keep Peter safe forever and ever and ever, both on land and on sea, she told the little fisherman.

When she had finished her task, Peter bent to kiss her, but he deliberately kept this kiss light.

"I'll never forget tonight," he told her. "It's been one of the happiest nights of my life, Marcie. I want you to know that."

"I'm going to break down and act like an idiot if you say another word," she warned him, dangerously close to tears.

"I'm going to break down and say things to you I shouldn't say right now," he told her in return.

He steered her toward the doorway. "I think," he said firmly, "it's time we joined the others."

CHAPTER 14

As Marcie dressed for dinner on Christmas Day, she fingered the silver seagull she was still wearing around her neck, and made the firm decision that she must not let her thoughts stray too far ahead. If she started to think about leaving Chatham and leaving Peter, she was certain to ruin Christmas for herself, and for him, too. I'm going to forget that there is any day but today! she told herself firmly.

She still fit very well into the Christmas green dress she had brought with her especially for this occasion, and the soaring silver seagull looked lovely against the deep, vibrant color, which not only was one of Marcie's favorites but was especially becoming to her. She brushed her hair until it shone and put on just enough makeup. The front doorbell was ringing and as she hurried downstairs, her father was welcoming Peter and his uncle and aunt.

Peter was wearing the same jacket and slacks he had worn to the carol concert last night, and Marcie suspected that his wardrobe was not too extensive; but he had added a bright red tie in honor of the holiday, and the little Gloucester fisherman showed up beautifully against it.

His eyes glowed with admiration as he looked at her, and she wished that she had the nerve to walk right over and kiss him in front of everyone — but she didn't.

May Higgins was wearing a red dress that seemed to bring color to her pale cheeks, and she looked happier today; and as Will Higgins joined her parents in a pre-dinner drink even he seemed to have caught some of the Christmas spirit.

The one discordant note, Marcie thought, was the bandage still in place on Peter's forehead. Every time she looked at it she was reminded of the attack on him, and of the fact that even though this was Christmas there was still a shadow over the Higgins family and Peter. It was more than a cloud of suspicion, too. The attack on Peter had proved that this particular shadow could materialize out of the unknown to assume a sinister shape that she didn't even like to contemplate.

After dinner, with the others protesting that they were too full to even move, Peter and Marcie put on warm woolen jackets and a knit caps and wound long wool scarves around their necks; Peter insisted that Marcie also put on some wool mittens which, he said, kept your hands warmer than gloves.

Outside, the bite of the air at first seemed icy, and Peter told her that the trick was to walk *into* the wind; then on the return trek, when you were tired, the wind would be at your back and actually help push you along, rather than fight you.

Walking into the wind led them down the beach in the direction away from the shack, and Marcie had the feeling that if it were not for the fact that Peter realized this he might not have given her his elemental lesson in weather lore. She suspected that he had no intention of letting her get near the late Howard Flynn's beach house.

They walked silently, holding hands. Then Peter said, "Somehow, you and your mother coming over to the house to see me after I'd been hurt broke the ice. Even Uncle Will has let down, you can see that; a couple of days ago nothing would have made me believe he'd go anywhere for Christmas dinner. It brought a real lump to my throat when I watched him just now, sitting there drinking coffee with your father. He was actually smiling."

"I noticed."

"This has broken the ice with Aunt May, too. But something quite different has happened in the course of that, Marcie."

There was a tone to his voice that caused her to look up at him questioningly.

"What do you mean?" she asked.

"Well, since last August Aunt May has been carrying a very heavy burden," Peter said. "I suspected it, I could see her getting thinner and more tense right before my eyes. I tried to talk to her time and time again, but her mouth was shut tighter than a clam's. Now, somehow, she's found

138

that she can't keep her secret any longer. Last night after I got home from your place. Uncle Will was asleep, but she was waiting up."

"Yes?"

"Well . . . she told me what it is she's been keeping to herself all this time, and nearly going crazy in the process."

"What?" Marcie demanded.

"The afternoon Howard Flynn was killed, right after he went down to check out the boat because of the hurricane warnings, Uncle Will wasn't home at all, like I thought he was. Uncle Will was out by himself in the storm, at just about the time Howard Flynn was murdered!"

CHAPTER 15

Marcie stared at Peter, horrified. Christmas and all its beauty seemed suddenly to have turned into a nightmare.

She said, "Peter, don't you think your aunt must be mistaken? You yourself said that when you got back from Woods Hole that afternoon, your aunt was home and your uncle was resting."

"That's right," Peter agreed. "He was lying on the couch in the living room, and Aunt May was fixing supper on the Coleman stove. I told you the power was out for several hours."

He frowned, and went on. "When Aunt May told me Howard Flynn had stopped by and said he'd go down and see to the boat, I didn't think any more about it. It never occurred to me that Uncle Will hadn't been right there in the house all afternoon. I knew the trouble he'd been having with his back. His doctor had warned him that if he didn't take care of himself he'd be in for a long hospital siege, and I know Uncle Will. He would do anything to avoid that! It's the one warning that would keep him down!"

"But why would he have ignored the doctor's advice and gone out?" Marcie demanded.

"I don't know how to answer that," Peter admitted. "Aunt May says it was because he was worried about the *May-Bee*. He didn't trust Flynn." Peter shook his head. "Whether that's the whole answer or not, I don't know."

Peter stared out at the gray water and watched a gull soaring across the sky. He said, "I never thought to ask Aunt May any questions the day of the storm, Marcie. I just took things as they were when I got home. The fact of the matter was that they had let school out in Chatham early that day, because of the hurricane warnings — and I suppose I should have realized that. In other words, Aunt May got home a couple of hours ahead of her usual time. Meanwhile, I had left Woods Hole, as I've told you, and I had quite a time making it back. I think it took me at least twice the usual driving time to get home; I'd say I was on the road the better part of two hours.

"Well, now Aunt May tells me that actually Uncle Will didn't get home very long before I did. That's why he was stretched out on the couch in the parlor, and why he seemed so tired. His back really *was* bothering him.

"They weren't trying to hide anything from me, not then. Aunt May had taken Uncle Will's wet clothes down and hung them up in the cellar to dry. She said he was soaked to the skin when he got in. I never noticed, because I hung my own things to dry out in an enclosed porch we have off the kitchen.

"The wind was really howling by then. I got a flashlight and went all through the house to be sure everything was closed tight that could be closed tight. The power was out, and Uncle Will was hoping the painkiller he'd taken for his back would hurry up and work. It wasn't a time to think about asking a lot of questions, especially if there didn't seem to be anything to ask questions *about*.

"Aunt May was out in the kitchen, as I remember it, when I came in," Peter continued, frowning as he tried to recall the exact scene. "I stopped in the parlor doorway long enough to ask Uncle Will about the boat before I went and changed into dry clothes. He said Howard Flynn had stopped by and said he was on his way down to look after her, so that was that. Otherwise, I would have gone on down to the pier myself.

"Neither Aunt May nor Uncle Will mentioned his having been out when Aunt May got home. She says now she was upset when she came in and he wasn't there, because she was worried about his back, but she's used to Uncle Will; she knows from experience that he's a hard man to keep down under any circumstances.

"When he did come back, he told her Flynn had come by earlier and promised to take care of the boat, and he was glad enough to go along with the idea at first because his back was giving him the devil. But later, Aunt May says, he got to wondering whether Flynn really had gone down to the fish pier, as he said he would, or if maybe he'd stopped off at the Buoy Bar on the way and had a couple, which might have been more than enough to take his mind off any business, if nature followed its usual course.

"Anyway — so Uncle Will told Aunt May — this began to bother him and he decided he'd better go down and take a look at the *May-Bee* himself, just to make certain she was all right. He drove the pickup truck over to the pier. He told Aunt May that when he got to the pier he found Flynn had been there and taken care of everything. By then there was no one else around. The rest of the fishermen had headed for cover."

"So no one else saw your uncle at the pier?" Marcie asked.

Peter nodded reluctantly. "That's the bad part of it. I know Uncle Will. I know it's exactly what he would have done. He wouldn't have trusted Flynn to look after the *May-Bee*. He couldn't have rested, bad back or no, unless he made sure himself that she was okay."

Peter shook his head. "When I think of it now," he told her, "it seems to me I should have realized there was something funny about the whole thing. I should have known that Uncle Will would have gone down to the pier himself, if he could so much as crawl."

"Peter," Marcie said, "aren't you blaming yourself unnecessarily? I mean, what difference would it have made if you *had* known?"

Peter looked at her soberly. "I could have alibied for him, Marcie. I would have said I went down to the pier with him, that we were down there together."

"As I understand it," Marcie said, "Chief Bearse has his suspicions about your own story, as it is."

"Yes, that's right, he has. He checked the time I left Woods Hole, and there's no doubt it took me a long while to get back here. He knows what the weather conditions were, though." Peter shrugged. "I suppose you can only say it's my word against his theories."

"Well, regardless of that, your aunt did give your uncle an alibi," Marcie pointed out.

"Yes, and obviously the police didn't believe her. That's the crazy part of it. *They* didn't believe Uncle Will was home at the time of Howard Flynn's murder and *I* did!" Peter spoke bitterly. "I only wish Aunt May had trusted me enough to tell me sooner about this."

"I can see why she didn't," Marcie said thoughtfully. "I can imagine that she didn't want to get you into this any deeper than you already are. As it is she's probably been worried to death all these weeks thinking that someone would turn up who did see your uncle out in the storm that day."

"That's what worries me," Peter said. "Suppose someone did, and they've told the police, and the police are just sort of sitting on the whole thing."

"Peter, you don't actually think your uncle was with Howard Flynn that afternoon, do you?"

144

Peter's gaze was stony. "Are you asking me if I think Uncle Will killed Flynn?" he demanded.

"Of course not. But if they did meet and anyone saw them together it could be very bad for him," Marcie said. "It does seem that if that were so and the police knew it they would . . . well, they would have arrested him by now," she added reluctantly.

They had turned and were walking back now, the wind at their backs, helping them along. Marcie said suddenly, "It seems to me that everyone is forgetting one of the most important things of all."

"What do you mean?"

"The reason why," Marcie said. "I guess if you wanted to sound like a TV detective you'd call it the motive. I don't believe your uncle killed his partner, so please don't get the wrong impression when I say what I'm going to say. But I think if you start asking yourself the question of who might have had a good reason to kill Howard Flynn, maybe some sort of an answer will start coming to you."

"I've gone through all that, Marcie," Peter told her. "I've gone over it again and again and again. Flynn wasn't a man who made any great waves, as far as I've been able to tell. True, no one seemed to like him, but I can't say I've found anyone who hated him enough to kill him, or seems to have had any reason for killing him. Nothing obvious, certainly.

"He and Uncle Will quarreled a lot before he was killed, and that does look bad. Uncle Will was getting more and more uptight about the *May-Bee*. It was August; he knew it was just a matter of time until we got into cold-weather fishing, winter storms and all the rest of it, and he knew that a lot needed to be done to the boat to make her really seaworthy. A couple of times, I know my uncle was honestly afraid they wouldn't make it back, and do you know, I don't think Flynn gave a damn. He had the *May-Bee* heavily insured — Tom Chardwell told Uncle Will about that — so if she had gone down he could have collected a pretty penny."

"What about your uncle?"

"Let's face it, Uncle Will has been a poor businessman," Peter admitted. "The insurance was in Flynn's name. That's one reason why I detest Chardwell so much. He was representing both of them at the time the partnership was drawn up, but obviously he weighed everything in Flynn's favor, and I think he's still concentrating mainly on Flynn's estate when he's supposed to be acting for Uncle Will."

"You said Howard Flynn had a cousin in California who is supposed to inherit everything?"

"Yes, if they can find him. He was Flynn's next of kin, according to Chardwell."

"Suppose they can't find this cousin? What will happen?"

"I'm not sure, Marcie. I think at some point everything probably will be liquidated, including the *May-Bee*, and then the money will go to the state or something, unless someone else can come forward and prove a blood relationship with

146

Flynn. I haven't spoken to Chardwell myself, but maybe I should. I felt it was really up to Uncle Will."

"Do you think there could be another heir, Peter?"

"I doubt it. Certainly they would have spoken up by now, if there were. If Flynn's property were liquidated, of course, Uncle Will would be entitled to forty-five percent of whatever came in from the sale of the *May-Bee*. But that's another problem. If the *May-Bee* were sold in the condition she's in now, she would bring only a fraction of what she'd be worth if she were repaired properly. That's what really gets me. No matter how this turns out, Uncle Will stands to be the loser!"

They walked the rest of the way back to Marcie's grandmother's house slowly, holding hands but not saying much more, their Christmas spirit understandably dampened by the thought of Willis and May Higgins's problems, which were to a large extent Peter's problems as well.

Although Marcie didn't voice her fear aloud to him, she found it overwhelmingly frightening to think that there was still someone around who had murder in his heart. The attempt on Peter's life could have had a far more serious result than it did, and as she thought about this she shuddered.

Peter pressed her hand tighter. "Cold?" he asked her.

"No," she said, and then admitted honestly,

"I'm frightened for you." She looked up at him, her hazel eyes revealing even more than she realized. "I can't bear to think of anything else happening to you," she said softly, "and until this thing is solved neither you nor your aunt nor your uncle will really be safe, Peter."

"I know that," he said grimly, "but you can be sure I'll have my personal radar working from now on."

"That's easy to say," she told him. "The whole thing is, whoever sneaked up behind you the other day must be pretty desperate, Peter. Why, I wonder? Why was he after *you?*"

"He — or it could be a she, you know, Marcie — must think I know a lot more than I do," Peter admitted.

"You think it could be a woman?"

"Flynn was killed with a fisherman's knife, and they are pretty easily available around here," he told her. "A lot of these Cape Cod women are pretty strong, too, and it wouldn't have taken any tremendous strength. The attack was such a total surprise.

"As for me, the doctors figure I was probably hit with a heavy wooden stick of some sort — they found a few splinters in my hair. Again, you can find a hunk of wood almost anyplace, and a woman could have struck that blow, too."

"Was there a woman in Howard Flynn's life?"

"Not that I know of," Peter admitted. "If there was, it might have been some sort of high school affair or something. It seems to me half the romances in Chatham start in high school. Obvi-

148

ously, that would be way before my time so, if Flynn ever did have a girl he was serious about, I've certainly never heard anything about it."

He took her by the shoulders and shook her gently. "Look," he said, "it's Christmas, Marcie, and we've said enough about all of this. More than enough! Let's go back in."

Marcie, at her grandmother's suggestion, played some Christmas songs on the old square piano in the back parlor after Peter and his aunt and uncle had gone, but she did so with an empty feeling, purely to please Grandmother Davies.

It had, in so many ways, been a wonderful Christmas, but it had left an unfortunate echo. It was an echo of worry, really — worry about Peter, primarily.

Marcie could not shut out the thought of someone sneaking after him across the dunes the other day, just as the previous August he had crept through the fog to attack and kill Howard Flynn. The all-important question loomed again: Why?

Why had whoever killed Howard Flynn felt impelled to stalk Peter and to attack him, not with a knife this time, but with a heavy, wooden weapon that could easily have been just as lethal?

As she played, Marcie's fingers suddenly clashed in a chord that was completely off-key. She started quickly to play again, before anyone could voice a protest, and for the next few minutes she managed to skip from one song to another. Then she simply had to stop.

The answer had come to her, and it seemed so simple that she couldn't imagine why Peter hadn't voiced it.

Peter had been on his way to the beach shack when he was attacked; he said that this was the first opportunity he had had to go back there since the afternoon he had intercepted Marcie when she was admittedly snooping. Now it seemed obvious to her that Peter had been attacked because there was something of such significance in the shack the murderer could not risk letting Will Higgins's nephew come upon it.

Somehow Marcie got through the rest of that Christmas Eve with her family, pleading sleepiness as an excuse at so early an hour that it made her father's eyebrows rise slightly. She hugged each of her family in turn, and thanked them again for her gifts, for the wonderful day, and for asking Peter and his aunt and uncle to share it with them.

But once upstairs in bed with the colorful old patchwork quilt pulled snugly around her, she lay awake for a long time, staring into the darkness, wide-eyed, as she plotted what she was going to do.

CHAPTER 16

Mr. Williams was taking a morning plane from Hyannis to Boston, where he would catch a direct flight to Washington. Marcie drove over to the airport with her mother to see him off.

Much of the Christmas snow had already melted, because it was getting foggy out and fog always caused snow to melt, at least fog in Chatham did; something about the salt in it, Ella had said vaguely.

Chatham really was the "fog factory" of Cape Cod, Marcie decided, once they had left the town behind them. Although it was gray and rather raw in Hyannis, visibility was good and Mr. Williams's plane had no difficulty in taking off.

On the way back from the airport, Marcie wondered if Peter and his uncle had tried to go out fishing this morning, or if the creeping fog was keeping them in. Fog, Ella had said, usually got worse before it got better.

Marcie thought about Willis Higgins, who had kept the *May-Bee* going these past few years by putting a large part of his own profits back into the boat, despite his partner's refusal to share in his burden. Further, Marcie knew, Uncle Will had helped Peter financially during those first two years at the university before he was given the scholarship that he had been unable to use. Now the Higginses were also being charged what Peter considered unusually large legal fees by Thomas Chardwell. None of this seemed right!

It came to Marcie that once a person was forced into a corner it was very hard to fight one's way out. This was what had been happening to Will Higgins for a long time now.

Back in Chatham, they had turkey sandwiches and hot tea for lunch, and then both Mrs. Williams and Mrs. Davies announced that they were tired. Marcie quickly agreed that she was, too.

"It's after-Christmas letdown," Ella said sagely, trying to tempt them with the choice of either mince pie or nut cake, only to be refused by all three of them. "You get all keyed up toward the holiday, then once it's over it's like letting the air out of a balloon."

Naps were in order, Mrs. Davies decreed, and she let Ella wheel her chair back to the small, first-floor bedroom she had been using since her fall.

When Ella returned she said, as if the mere idea were outrageous, "I almost think I might put my head down for a spell, myself."

Marcie hoped that her relief at this statement of Ella's wasn't visible, because she was well aware of how sharp Ella was, and this was one time she didn't want the housekeeper to know what she was up to!

The fog was continuing to creep in; it slithered across the beachfront, touching the windows with pale gray, wraithlike fingers.

Marcie waited until she was sure that her mother, her grandmother, and Ella had all settled in for their naps, and then she crept down the old staircase, praying that the big, wide boards wouldn't creak as she crossed the parlor, carrying her heavy wool jacket, her long scarf, and her knitted cap with her. She quickly slipped them on, remembering to put on mittens, too, and then she opened the front door carefully, leaving it unlocked. She intended to complete her errand and be back before anyone woke up.

She walked quickly along the beach, knowing her way this time. It didn't seem nearly as far as it had the first day before she rounded the point, and soon the sagging old beach shack loomed up in front of her, its one blank window staring opaquely through the mist.

She wasted no time in wondering whether or not there was anyone inside. She was certain that there wasn't, and although it was tempting to go up the steps that led to the top of the dunes and look across—just in case someone might be keeping an eye on the place—she forced herself to march right toward the sagging door, keeping as close as possible to the walls of the shack.

Peter had been attacked on top of the dunes,

she reminded herself. Howard Flynn had been *killed* on that same path, which ran across the top of the dunes to the street beyond. There was no reason, however, for anyone to think that someone might approach the shack via the beach itself.

Grandmother Davies was one of the few people who lived year round in a house right on the beachfront, and anyone who knew her also knew that she was laid up with a broken leg. Moreover, what interest would seventy-year-old Mrs. Davies, a relatively wealthy woman in her own right, have in the contents of the late Howard Flynn's tumbledown old shack?

Most of the other beachfront houses were boarded up, at least the two near her grandmother's house were. Admittedly, Marcie had not gone very far around the far side of the point, but she doubted very much that anyone connected with Howard Flynn would have lived there, either in the summer or all year around. From what Ella had told her, most of the people with beachfront property deplored Flynn's unsightly shack and had been seeking some legal way that might force him to tear it down.

No, Marcie told herself, as she approached the sagging door, if the murderer were keeping a watch on the shack he was doing it from somewhere up above, past the dunes. Even though she had yet to walk up those steps herself, she was certain just from looking that only the roof of the shack would be visible from the top.

She kept telling herself this, wrapping herself

up in her certainty that no one could be spying on her as if it were some kind of security blanket. She tentatively pushed the door open, and the horrible, screeching sound it made tore at her nerves so that she started shaking despite herself.

She was strongly tempted to turn and run back down the beach. In fact, it seemed to her that nothing could possibly be as wonderful at this moment as the safe comfort of the kitchen in her grandmother's house, with Ella busy at the stove making a big cup of hot cocoa to warm her up.

Standing on the threshold, she forced herself to think of Peter, to think *hard* about Peter, and after a moment this steadied her.

The inside of the shack smelled worse than ever, and the place looked even more grimy and deplorable than it had the first time she had seen it. Evidently cold weather didn't affect the spiders. They had kept on with their work, and the network of cobwebs looked like something out of a late night TV horror story.

Marcie realized that she should have brought a flashlight. The lamp on the desk was kerosene, but she found a pack of matches nearby and was about to strike a light when she stopped to remember that a lighted window could be singularly visible. Although she was reasonably certain that even this couldn't be seen from the top of the dunes, there was no point in taking chances.

She hated to touch the grubby bedclothes on the bunk the late Howard Flynn had last slept in, but she resolutely dragged a blanket over to the grimy window and draped it completely. The wooden edges stuck out sufficiently so that it was easy to fasten it securely enough to stay up as long as she was in the shack.

She duplicated this performance with the kitchen window, gasping from the stench in that room, and resolved that once home again she would wash her hands with antiseptic before she even touched anything else. Even the feel of the blankets was disgusting, they were so dirty.

She looked around, wondering where to begin. Where would an old miser keep his secrets? she asked herself. If he had any secrets.

She turned her attention first to the paper carton underneath the table where the lamp stood. Evidently this table had served Howard Flynn both as a place to work on his accounts and as a place to eat. There was still a crusting of something that looked like dried-up mustard along one edge of it.

The carton was full of old newspapers and rags, crumpled paper napkins, and a similar assortment of what could only be called trash. She realized that Flynn had probably kept such odds and ends to use in helping him start the wood stove, which stood in the kitchen and must have been his only source of heat in winter.

There were no drawers in the table, nor was there a closet in the room. A few hooks along one wall held the miscellaneous assortment of coats and foul-weather gear that must have constituted the major part of Howard Flynn's wardrobe. Two overhead shelves were stacked with an assortment of folded shirts, flannel underwear, and a few pairs of socks.

Marcie had hoped that she would not have to go back into the kitchen again, but there was no alternative. Carrying the kerosene lamp with her, she made her way there, and as quickly as she could surveyed the shelves and even opened the malodorous refrigerator.

Then, holding her nose with the fingers of one hand and carrying the lamp in the other, she went back into the other room, convinced that there was no place in the kitchen where anyone could hide anything.

She stood in the center of the floor, literally drooping with disappointment. Was it possible that Howard Flynn really had had nothing to hide? Or had he kept his important papers in a bank, or turned them over for safekeeping to Thomas Chardwell, who had been his attorney as well as Willis Higgins's?

Marcie was about to give up when her eyes fell upon the disreputable old bunk bed. It stood quite high off the floor. There was surely room to store things underneath it, and in an instant she was beside it. She set the kerosene lamp down carefully; she didn't want to risk burning the place up, and kerosene lamps could be dangerous if you tilted them too far. Cringing slightly — the floor was as grubby as everything else and she expected a mouse, if not a rat, to come out and confront her at any moment — Marcie knelt down by the side of the bunk bed.

She threw back the covers and very carefully

positioned the lamp so it cast some light under the bed, not as much as she could have wished but enough to show if there was something there.

It was another cardboard box, flatter than the one under the table, and this one had a lid on it.

Marcie pulled it out, her hands trembling, and carried it across to the table, then brought the lamp back to its original position. In the circle of yellow light cast by the glowing kerosene wick, she pushed back the cardboard cover and the contents of the box were clearly revealed to her.

She didn't know what she had expected to see but this, certainly, was not it. There was a stack of what looked like the kind of composition books elementary school children use, except, she found as she opened one, Howard Flynn obviously had used them as ledgers.

He had listed absolutely everything he had ever bought: two postage stamps, a package of razor blades, a Sunday newspaper, a pound of coffee, some tobacco . . . the list went on and on, amazing in the precision of its detail.

The ledgers went back over a period of years and so did his checkbooks. The books themselves, containing only stubs, were secured by rubber bands. Canceled checks were kept in separate piles, also secured by rubber bands. Marcie glanced at the date on one check and saw that it went back fifteen years.

Under the checkbooks she found some old savings account books. She opened the first one and discovered that it went back *twenty* years. The second one surprised her. The last entry in it was dated early the previous August, but it was the final figure that made her eyes widen.

Howard Flynn had left a balance of over nine thousand dollars in that savings bank, and as she thumbed through the pages, Marcie noted that this particular account had been started a year ago the previous January.

It took only a moment to ascertain that, beginning that January and for the next twenty months, Flynn had deposited five hundred dollars in the account on the fifth day of each month, with unfailing regularity.

It came to Marcie that undoubtedly his next deposit would have been due on the fifth of last September, and she had no doubt at all that it would have been made — had he lived!

Was all of this money derived from the profits he made fishing with Will Higgins aboard the *May-Bee?* True, Flynn had lived alone, and his surroundings, his clothes — and everything she could learn about him — clearly indicated that he had been a miser. She suspected that the only money he had spent on anything beside the bare necessities had been his forays into the Buoy Bar, where there were occasions when he drank quite heavily.

Even then, though, he had evidently done his drinking alone.

Howard Flynn certainly had been a man without friends, apparently with no one at all who had even seemed to like him, let alone love him. As she looked around the squalid shack where he had lived, Marcie wished that this could have moved her to pity him, but it didn't

There was something about these records, something about the savings account book, that made her feel more than ever that the late Howard Flynn had been a most unsavory person. However, she could not just then have voiced a logical reason for feeling as she did.

The police surely must have searched Flynn's shack after his death. They must have found his box of old ledgers and checkbooks. Probably they had dismissed them as being of little consequence, knowing that Thomas Chardwell was Flynn's attorney, and assuming that Chardwell would have any records of significance in connection with his client's affairs.

If there were a secret in connection with Howard Flynn's past, it seemed to Marcie that it might very well lie somewhere within this miscellaneous bunch of old bank statements and canceled checks and savings books and records, but it would take time and study to ferret it out.

There was no possible way she could do it in the shack, which left only a single course of action possible.

Much as she disliked the thought of returning to the shack, she would have to come back again. This time she would bring her tote bag so she could take Flynn's papers back to her grandmother's house and find the opportunity to go through them thoroughly — without anyone, even Peter, being the wiser!

CHAPTER 17

Marcie glanced at her watch as she left the shack, carefully closing the screeching door behind her. It was a quarter to four, and she was afraid that by now her mother and her grandmother and Ella would all be up and about again.

The fog was closing in and she shivered. There was something so mysterious about the fog, something especially frightening about it when you had just been cooped up by yourself in a place like Howard Flynn's shack.

She wished she could ask Peter if it were possible that his uncle's partner could have banked five hundred dollars month after month, in a separate savings account. She knew, though, that she didn't dare, because she couldn't risk letting Peter know yet that she had stumbled on Flynn's secreted cardboard box.

Peter, she suspected, would be even more furious than her family if he knew she had gone back to the beach shack. He had warned her against doing this the very first time they met.

Now, as she passed the first of the shuttered summer houses on the way back to her grandmother's, she saw a figure looming ahead through the fog. For a moment she thought, that it must be Peter, that somehow he had suspected where she had gone and had followed her.

The person approaching her, however, was much shorter than Peter, and much too slender, and as the gap between them lessened she saw that it was Trudy Bailey, wearing yellow oilskin foul-weather gear.

Trudy, peering through the fog, called, "Marcie?"

"Yes," Marcie answered, and quickened her steps.

"I'm glad I started out the right way," Trudy said. "Ella Mayo told me she expected you'd gone for a walk while the rest of them were napping. I felt as if I should toss a coin when I started out to find you. It's hard to see very far ahead in this fog."

Marcie nodded. "Well, I'm glad you chose the right way," she said, tremendously relieved that she had left the beach shack when she did. She had no desire for Trudy Bailey or anyone else to know she had been there.

She shivered. "The dampness goes right through you, doesn't it?" she said. "Let's go on back to grandmother's and get something warm to drink."

The two girls were walking side by side now, and Trudy said, "I can't, Marcie. I shouldn't be here at all, really. We ran short on coffee and Dad sent me up to the market to get some. I decided to take a few extra minutes to come over, just to thank you."

"Thank me?"

"For the flowers and for coming the other night," Trudy said. "I wanted to call you yesterday, but I knew you'd be busy with your family on Christmas, and that Peter and his aunt and uncle were having dinner with you."

Marcie glanced quickly at Trudy. Did she just imagine it, or was there really a special sort of note in Trudy's voice when she mentioned Peter's name?

They had reached Grandmother Davies's house and Marcie said impulsively, "Trudy, I'm sure Ella already has a pot of tea made, if I know her. Come in, just for a few minutes. It won't make that much difference to your father."

"Well," Trudy hesitated, and finally yielded.

Marcie was right. Ella had made tea and had put out a plate of Christmas cookies, but her face was stern as Marcie entered the kitchen, with Trudy behind her.

"You haven't been fooling around Flynn's beach shack again, have you?" she asked, her flat Cape Cod accent sounding flatter than ever.

"Oh, Ella, don't be so suspicious," Marcie protested, which was neither an affirmation or a confirmation, but fortunately it mollified Ella for the moment.

The two girls drank their tea and Trudy ate two cookies, but she was obviously in a hurry. Marcie wished that she could make her linger a bit longer.

When Trudy had gone, Ella said, "Someone should give Tim Bailey a real talking to. There's no doubt he dotes on that girl, yet he works her much too hard in that coffee shop, if you ask me, and he doesn't seem to realize what he's doing to her. Sometimes I think his wife's death has made him kind of strange."

"You mean if Trudy's mother were alive, Trudy would still be at the conservatory?" Marcie asked.

"I should say so!" Ella said firmly. "Hilda Bailey was a lovely person, used to play the organ in church, she did; that's where Trudy got her musical talent from. It was Hilda who saw to it that Trudy studied voice and that she went to Boston to the conservatory. It's been pure selfishness on Tim's part, keeping her tied up down here since her mother died. If you ask me, he's got kind of a fixation on the girl." Ella shook her head. "Funny," she said, "the things folks do sometimes to the people they love the most. Doesn't seem to be any reason to a lot of it."

Dinner was a quiet affair that night, with just Marcie, her mother, and her grandmother at the big table. There still should have been holiday magic, but somehow there wasn't, and Marcie realized that this was primarily because the entire day had passed and she had heard nothing from Peter.

Now she was torn between wanting to hear from him and wanting to be free to attend to her own business, for she had already come to the conclusion that the only way she could possibly get the contents of that cardboard box out of Howard Flynn's place was to do it after dark.

She shrank from the thought of going to the shack alone at night, yet she knew she couldn't possibly walk in with her tote bag bulging in broad daylight without arousing her mother's and her grandmother's suspicions, to say nothing of Ella's.

Finally she determined that she would simply have to wait until the others were asleep before going out.

But as the evening went on, Marcie found her courage leaving her and she went to bed, angry with herself for failing to carry out her plans.

CHAPTER 18

The second day after Christmas reminded Marcie very much of the morning after her arrival on the Cape, when she had awakened to find the world outside her window damp and shrouded in fog.

Because it was so dank and miserable outside and she was so cozy underneath her old fashioned patchwork quilt, Marcie had overslept. She awakened to hear Ella stirring around in the kitchen downstairs, and knew what she had to do today. She had to sneak down to the beach shack and retrieve Howard Flynn's papers. Frightened or not, she had to go.

But how? There would be no excuse to go out and take a walk on a day like this, which meant that she would have to wait till dark, and again she shrank from the thought of this.

She wondered what Peter was doing. He had told her that they took advantage of bad weather to take care of odds and ends on the boat that needed repairing, and she supposed that he was down at the fish pier with his uncle. She would have borrowed her mother's car on some pretext or other and driven down to see him, except that she could not face up to the possibility of "bothering" Willis Higgins. He had been pleasant enough to her on Christmas, but she sensed that he didn't particularly encourage Peter's interest in her and wouldn't welcome her interfering with their work.

She moped around the house, writing some thank you letters to friends who had sent gifts via her father. Then she tried to read a book she would have enjoyed at another time, but simply couldn't concentrate on now.

She had thought briefly that it might make more sense if she and Peter went back to retrieve Flynn's papers and go over them together. But Peter might refuse flatly to go to the shack with her and, no doubt would, in fact, insist that she stay away.

More and more, she felt there must be an answer to at least a part of the puzzle surrounding Flynn's death in that box of old papers, and if so, she was going to find out what it was.

During the course of the afternoon, Mrs. Davies's doctor stopped by to see her. He told her to come in for X-rays within the next few days but added that he definitely didn't want her "cavorting around," even with her daughter and her granddaughter's help, until the weather was considerably better.

"Fog can make the roads pretty slick," he said, and added emphatically, "We're not taking any chances with you!"

As Dr. Swan was about to leave, Grandmother

Davies said, unexpectedly, "How is that cut on young Peter Doane's head coming along?"

"I took the stitches out this morning," Dr. Swan replied. "It's healing very nicely. There will be a scar, but not much of one. Peter's young enough, it'll fade out fairly well with time — and the whole thing could have been much worse."

There was a note to his voice as he said this that gave Marcie a chill.

It could indeed have been so much worse! Thinking about it only strengthened Marcie's resolution to get those papers out of Howard Flynn's shack and back to her own room, where she could study them in safety.

Actually, she told herself, a foggy night could be a help to her, as long as she was careful with her footing going along the beach. If possible, she would not use her flashlight at all until she was actually inside the house, so if anyone *was* watching from some place on top of the dunes they wouldn't be able to spot her.

It would take only a few seconds to transfer the contents of the cardboard box into her tote bag and to be off through the night again. It was simply a matter of being precise about it and not panicking, she told herself.

They were just about to sit down to the dinner table when the phone rang, and Ella came to the dining room door to announce that the call was for Marcie.

As she went to answer the phone, Marcie was certain that it must be Peter, and much as she wanted to see him she didn't want him coming over tonight. Time, she knew, was running out. If many more delays were thrown in her path, she never would get to the beach shack.

She tried to decide what to tell Peter that would not arouse Ella's suspicions, for she knew very well that even as Ella was carrying the creamed turkey into the dining room at least one of her ears would be concentrating on Marcie's conversation. But, when she said "Hello," the voice at the other end of the wire very definitely was not Peter's!

"Marcie," said Trudy Bailey, and she sounded very far away and thoroughly frightened. "Look, I'm calling from a phone booth and I've got to speak quickly. Marcie, you're in *terrible* danger! Whatever you do, don't go near that old shack on the beach where Howard Flynn used to live!"

And with that she hung up.

Ella, pausing in the act of transferring hot rolls from a baking pan to a serving dish, observed, "Well, that was short and sweet."

"Yes," Marcie said. "Trudy had to get back to work, she just had a minute to spare."

She joined her mother and her grandmother quickly before Ella could ask any more questions. As it happened, the evening's bridge guests came early and Ella was anxious to get away herself, so Trudy's call was — fortunately, from Marcie's point of view — forgotten.

With Ella gone, though, and her grandmother and her mother settled down in the parlor playing bridge with their friends, Marcie wandered out into the kitchen and sat down at the big round wooden table, thinking about Trudy's warning and wondering just what to make of it.

Trudy, she knew, had a rare opportunity to overhear things. Working as she did at the counter in Tim's Place, it would be an easy enough matter for her to listen in on conversations between the many fishermen who came there regularly.

What might she have heard? Surely whatever it was had seemed urgent enough that she had left her father's coffee shop to go and place a call from a public phone, and she had sounded absolutely terrified.

Still, it didn't make sense. How could she, Marcie Williams, possibly be in danger? No one knew that she had ever been in Howard Flynn's shack except Peter. And she had absolute faith in Peter.

It was possible, of course, that Peter had mentioned it to his uncle, had mentioned the scene of his initial encounter with her; but could she be in danger from Willis Higgins? Could Willis Higgins actually be guilty?

She didn't like the thought of this.

In any event, she told herself, the only sensible course now was to call Peter and ask him to go to the shack with her tonight, under cover of the fog. Then they could bring the papers back here. They could spread them out right on the kitchen table, for that matter. Once she had them in her possession, she didn't care whether her mother or

170

her grandmother or Ella or anyone else knew about them.

She picked up the phone book, found Willis Higgins's number, and dialed it. May Higgins answered the telephone, and when Marcie identified herself and asked to speak to Peter, May said that both he and his uncle were at a meeting of the fishermen's cooperative.

In response to Marcie's inquiry, she said she had no idea when they would be back, but she'd be happy to ask Peter to call Marcie if it wasn't too late.

"No," Marcie said, almost too quickly. "That is ... I'm sort of tired, and I think I may go to bed early. I'll get in touch with him tomorrow."

"Very well, dear," May Higgins replied. And that was that.

Marcie hung up the phone receiver, surprised to find that her fingers were trembling.

With Peter out, there was only one thing she could do.

She couldn't wait any longer. Trudy's call had only emphasized that time was running out.

She had to go to the beach shack, and she had to go *now*, even though it meant going alone.

Marcie slipped out the kitchen door, her tote bag clasped in one hand and her flashlight in the other. She closed the door very gently behind her, making sure it was unlocked, so that she would have no problem getting back into the house again.

As she cautiously made her way across the

strip of dry, bristly grass, finally reaching the sandy edge of the beach, the fog and the darkness seemed to close in about her in a kind of mutual, alien compact. She very nearly shrank away from both, yearning to run back through that kitchen door to the warmth and security of her grandmother's house.

But that would be the coward's way, she told herself as she kept on going, moving slowly and carefully, determined not to make a false step that could send her tumbling.

The tide was coming in. In just these few days she had learned to recognize the sound it made as it lapped toward the shore in a steady ebb and flow, each small thrust causing the water to rise just a bit higher. Marcie realized that by the time the tide was in full, there would not be very much space between the small mound on which the beach shack stood and the open water itself.

There was no moon tonight, no stars, nothing to guide her; and the thickening fog brushed her with entwining tentacles that gave her the eerie feeling it was trying to force her to go back — that even the winter fog itself disapproved of her errand.

She began to feel as if the fog was a real, tangible creature, and she chided herself for being ridiculously imaginative. She remembered that once, when she was a child, she had overheard an elderly aunt telling her mother rather tartly, "Marcie has too much imagination for her own good!" She couldn't remember what her mother had replied, but right now she wished she weren't inclined to be quite so imaginative, that she could accept the fog as simply fog, without endowing it with any mystical, spectral qualities.

It seemed a long time before she dimly glimpsed a shape to her right, the first of the two shuttered summer houses. Then she passed the second house shape. She knew now that very shortly she would be rounding the point, and her footsteps began to falter.

She stood stock still for quite a long moment, just listening. But the fog was noiseless; she heard only the steady lapping of the incoming tide.

At least, she thought, I'm alone out here. There's no one else around, Marcie. There's no one else.

She came to the point, and she rounded it; now she could sense the shack ahead of her almost more than she could see it. She was careful with her footing as she mounted the stone slab step; she pushed, and then heard the screeching noise that meant the door was swinging inward.

She stepped inside, nearly reeling from the terrible smell which seemed even worse than before, but remembering to carefully close the door behind her, so that as little light as possible would be visible outside when she switched on her flashlight.

Now, with the flashlight on, she sped across the grimy little room to the bunk bed, knelt beside it and quickly drew out the cardboard box. Working so quickly that she started dropping things in her haste, she transferred its contents to her tote bag. This finished, she quickly shone the flashlight around the floor to be sure that she had retrieved everything, and found that she had — with the exception of a single packet of letters, banded together with a blue elastic.

Letters! They must have fallen out from the midst of some of the ledgers and bundles of checks, and her curiosity about them was overwhelming. She yearned to stop and read at least one of them, but there would be time enough later for that, she warned herself. The thing to do now was to get home!

She thrust the letters in the tote bag with all the other papers, quickly made her way to the door, and remembered to extinguish the flashlight before she opened it.

She felt for the edge of the stone slab cautiously and had just stepped off it and was starting up the beach again when she heard the voice coming out of the fog. It was a hoarse voice, a hideous voice; it was, in fact, as if the winter fog itself suddenly was speaking to her.

"So you *would* pry!" the voice hissed.

Marcie tried to turn, tried to peer through the darkness toward the source of this horrible whisper. But even as she started to move she felt something sudden and sharp and knew only that she was slumping down onto the sand, completely at the mercy of the murderer!

CHAPTER 19

The world had changed into an enormous cauldron of milk. The milk, Marcie thought, was very much like fog, except that there was a warmth to its whiteness. She was almost comfortable swimming in its gentle, opaque softness until it began to swirl around her, and then that hurt.

Someone said, "Take it easy. Oh, my God, Marcie! Dearest, dearest Marcie!"

A shape emerged through the milk, coming closer and closer and closer and Marcie saw that it was Peter. His blue eyes were so intense that she felt as if they were stabbing her, and for a moment she had to shut her own eyes, as she heard Peter say, desperately, "Marcie!"

He sounded so totally helpless, so distraught, that she found her voice again.

"Peter," she said, quite clearly. "I'm all right."

The soft, warm milk was ebbing away, and now she could see other people: her mother, her grandmother, and Dr. John Swan.

Her mother started to say, "Marcie," and sounded as if she were going to cry.

Her grandmother said, "Doctor . . ."

Dr. Swan smiled down at Marcie before he answered.

"She's a chip off the old block, Mrs. Davies," he said then. "Maybe not *quite* as tough as her grandmother — but almost."

Her head hurt, it really hurt, but her vision was clear, and she could also see Ella, and Willis Higgins, and May Higgins. Willis looked just as worried as all the rest of the people around her. For a reason she couldn't fully understand, this made her very happy.

She tried to find her voice again but now it seemed to be eluding her, and when she did speak the sound emerged more like a croak than anything else.

She said, "The whisper came right out of the fog."

It was Peter who answered her. "I know," he said softly. "I was there. I heard it."

"*You* were there?" She tried to raise her head, but this proved to be impossible.

"Yes. We got home earlier than Aunt May expected us and she said you had called and sounded upset. I phoned here, and your mother couldn't find you and . . . well, I put things together. I hoped I was wrong, but I was very much afraid you'd gone just where you *did* go! I had sense enough to tell Aunt May to get hold of the police and then I made tracks, believe me. I came down across the dunes, but at that I got there barely in time!"

"Okay," Dr. Swan said, and he looked surprisingly stern. "That's enough. Peter, do you think you could help me carry Marcie upstairs? Then we'll let her mother get her into bed, and after that I'm going to give her something that will help her sleep through the night."

Very briefly, he smiled down at Marcie again. "Tomorrow will be time enough for talking," he told her.

Peter carried her upstairs by himself, and even though her head hurt, even though things were hazy, there was such strength and warmth and comfort in his arms that she knew, whatever happened, somehow everything had to be all right.

Then Ella and her mother undressed her and put her into bed, and they carefully tucked the patchwork quilt up around her. After that, Dr. Swan came in, gave her an injection, and said, "I really hadn't intended to permit any visitors tonight, but I'm afraid Peter Doane will break the door down if I don't let him in. You can only stay a minute though, Peter, understand?"

"Yes, sir," Peter said, his voice low and subdued.

He came to the bedside and knelt down so that his face was close to the level of her face, and he kissed her very gently.

"The doctor's right," he said. "Tomorrow will be time enough for talking. But I do have to tell you one thing now, before you go to sleep tonight. I want you to know that I love you very much."

She couldn't find her voice, but she did manage to make her fingers creep across the quilt until they found his fingers, and he was still holding her hand when she fell asleep.

Late the next afternoon Dr. Swan paid Marcie another visit and told her that although her head was going to be pretty sore for a couple of days she was a very lucky young woman. She would not even have a scar to show for the incident. She was permitted to go downstairs, and she curled up on the couch in the parlor. Her mother and her grandmother went discreetly into the back parlor and even shut the door in between, so that Peter could tell her in his own way what had to be told.

It was not easy, even though the cloud of suspicion had been lifted from his Uncle Will's shoulders and there would be a whole new life ahead for Will and May Higgins.

"Things have moved so quickly it's incredible," Peter said. "This morning Uncle Will and I went over to the courthouse, in Orleans, and had a talk with the judge there, who has known Uncle Will for years. As a result, Uncle Will has fired Tom Chardwell, who has been feathering his own nest all these weeks and doing nothing for Uncle Will at all!

"We've discovered, among other things, that Chardwell knew Howard Flynn's cousin in California died five years ago. He was holding up this information, and I think by the time we get through with this case he may be disbarred. A

178

charlatan like that certainly shouldn't be practicing law.

"It develops that under the terms of the contract Uncle Will had with Flynn, the *May-Bee* is now entirely his, and he can also put in a claim against Flynn's estate for the share of money put into her over the years that should have been paid by Flynn. Flynn should have paid the greater part of all these expenses, as a matter of fact, because he owned the majority interest in the boat."

Peter stretched, and ate another one of the brownies Ella had placed on the table by the side of his chair. He said, "Uncle Will has pretty well decided that he's going to put the *May-Bee* in good shape over the rest of the winter, with my help, and then he's going to sell her. With the money he can get for her, he'll be able to set himself up in a marine supply business. There's a big demand for that sort of business around here, Uncle Will is well known and well liked, and he should do very well. It's a perfect solution for him; with his bad back commercial fishing really is out for him, and I think he and Aunt May are both going to be a great deal happier this way."

"What will you do?" Marcie asked him.

He smiled down at her. "I'll be going back to college in the fall, Marcie. I'm going to stick it out through the winter and spring with Uncle Will because he still needs me. After that, though, I'll be a free agent."

Marcie said slowly, "That's wonderful. The whole thing is wonderful, about you and your

179

uncle and aunt, and I'm glad your uncle finally realized that Thomas Chardwell was just using him."

"When he saw those various bankbooks and other documents you'd stashed in your tote bag, he *knew* it," Peter told her.

She looked across at him, and for the first time Peter evaded her eyes.

"All right," she said. "You can't keep it from me forever, Peter. What else did you discover among Howard Flynn's papers, and who were the letters from?"

Peter sighed. He said, ruefully, "This is the bad part, and I know I've got to tell you the rest of it but I hate to, Marcie. You remember you had asked if there had been a woman in Howard Flynn's life, and I said if there had been it must go way back to a high school sweetheart, or something like that?"

"Yes, I do remember that."

"Well . . . Flynn *did* have a high school sweetheart. She was a lovely girl; she came from a good family and they didn't approve of Flynn, so the romance was a carefully kept secret. I guess it really got heavy about their last year in high school, and . . . well, finally she wrote him that she was pregnant.

"The letters are pretty pathetic. She started in by telling him she was pretty sure, and then she began to beg him to marry her, right then and there, so no one would ever have to know she'd gotten in trouble. She knew if they ran away and got married it would make her family furious,

180

but felt it wouldn't be half as bad then as it would be later, when they found out she was going to have Flynn's baby.

"Evidently Flynn never even answered her. She kept on writing, and the letters got more and more desperate. Then, finally, she wrote one very defiant letter in which she said she wouldn't be bothering him again because she was going to marry someone else. She said that when the baby was born, she was going to let this 'someone else' believe the child was his. First babies, she said, were often born a little bit early. She said she had known old Dr. Sanders ever since she was a baby herself; she was going to him, and she knew he would help her and keep her secret. Evidently he did, too, because that's the way it worked out. Dr. Sanders died quite a few years ago, and I'd say he went to the grave without ever saying anything about this."

Marcie moistened her lips, hating to hear the answer to the question she was going to ask.

"Who was it, Peter?" she asked him.

"Trudy Bailey's mother. Hilda Bailey. She was a wonderful person, everyone loved her. I guess Tim Bailey had always been in love with her, but she never paid any attention to him. When she started to, he was quick enough to propose and they ran off and got married secretly, even before they were graduated from high school.

"Hilda's parents were very strict. Evidently she sold Tim on the idea that they would never consent to her getting married until she was older, but that if the two of them ran off they'd almost certainly accept it. At least they wouldn't put her through the misery of an annulment, she told him. Anyway, they did run off, and in due course Trudy was born 'early.'"

"And, of course, Howard Flynn always knew that Trudy was actually his child."

"Yes," Peter nodded. "Fortunately, Trudy took after her mother; I understand her resemblance to Hilda is astounding. As she grew up, Tim doted on her more and more, and after her mother's death she got to be a regular obsession with him. Flynn saw this and decided to take advantage of it. Greed always was his downfall.

"He told Tim that unless he paid him five hundred dollars on a certain day each month, he would show Trudy the letters proving she was his child. He claimed he kept them in a safe deposit box. That's why Tim never searched the shack, and why he went through mental agony for weeks.

"Anyway, Tim started making the payments, but his wife's last illness had cost a small fortune, far more than his insurance covered. He began to get in a real trap and begged Flynn to let up on him, to let him make smaller payments. Flynn wouldn't. Finally it got to be more than Tim Bailey could handle. It got to him mentally. He was pretty much on the brink by the time he sneaked across the dunes that night and stabbed Flynn.

"Then he began to get suspicious about me. I think," Peter said honestly, "it was because I talked too much. I knew the police had searched

Flynn's shack, and I can't blame them for not lingering. They had found the box with all the canceled checks and stuff, but when they went through it there didn't seem to be anything that meant anything. You see, there was a hollowed-out place in one of those ledgers where he kept the letters taped in. I think the tape must have dried out, Marcie, and the letters got loose."

"I dropped some of the ledgers, I was in such a hurry," Marcie admitted. "That's when the letters fell out on the floor."

Peter nodded. "That explains it. Initially, Flynn had them fairly well camouflaged. Anyway, I've always felt there was something in that shack that would be a clue to the murder, and I probably said so — maybe to Trudy, maybe to someone else when I was having coffee in Tim's Place. That afternoon before I started out for the shack, I mentioned to Trudy that I had an errand to do before I went home, and I guess maybe Tim overheard and got suspicious about it, probably from my own tone of voice, so he followed me and attacked me. You know, I don't think he wanted to kill me. I don't think he wanted to really harm you. He just had to stop both of us."

"Trudy tried to warn me yesterday," Marcie said.

"I know. Her father got pretty angry when she was late getting back the other afternoon after he sent her to get coffee. He was evidently harping on it yesterday when she started out somewhere, and she told him she had gone over to thank you for the flowers and met you on the beach. She said that suddenly the look in her father's eyes terrified her, and he started asking questions about you, and if you had been anywhere near Flynn's shack. Trudy was really frightened. I think at that point she *knew*, Marcie, and she felt she had to warn you."

"How terrible for her!"

"Yes, it is. By then, of course, Tim's first thought was to get to the shack himself and search it, as well as look out for both you and me. He was convinced we were highly dangerous to him — and I guess we were."

"What will happen to Tim Bailey, Peter?"

"They've sent him up to the State Mental Hospital in Bridgewater, and the psychiatrists there will examine him to determine what his mental condition really is. It's too early to say."

"What about Trudy?"

"Hilda Bailey had a sister who lives in Boston. She has wanted Trudy to make her home with her for years, and Trudy stayed with her when she was going to the conservatory. Chief Bearse drove her up to her aunt's himself yesterday; he's a pretty decent man, actually, Marcie. That's the best place for Trudy for the time being. Later, I think she'd like to see both of us, but right now she's better off away from Chatham."

"I hope some day — no matter what happens — she'll go back to her music," Marcie said.

"I think she will."

"And you'll be going back to school yourself. Some day you'll be a famous marine biologist," Marcie said. Somehow the thought of this made her feel very lonely just now. She realized her head was beginning to really hurt and that she was getting very tired.

Peter reached over and took the crocheted afghan her grandmother kept draped on the back of the couch, and he drew it over Marcie.

"And some day," he said gently, "you will be a world-famous lawyer! But just now, dearest Marcie, you're going to take a nap."

CHAPTER 20

At five minutes before midnight on New Year's Eve, Frederick Williams went to the kitchen door and called, "Ella! Will you stop fussing with the first food we're going to eat in the New Year and come in here and have a glass of champagne with the rest of us?"

Ella, grumbling only slightly, joined the others around the twinkling Christmas tree and accepted the glass Mr. Williams handed her.

"Never did go much for this bubbly stuff," she protested, but nevertheless she was smiling.

Mrs. Davies, Mr. and Mrs. Williams, Will and May Higgins, Peter, and Marcie were already holding their champagne and, as the chimes on the old grandfather clock in the corner began to ring out, glasses clicked, champagne was sipped, and then everyone was kissing everyone else.

Peter took his time about releasing Marcie, and her cheeks were flushed as she looked up to see her mother's and father's eyes upon her, but they were smiling. In fact, everyone was smiling.

"Well," Mr. Williams said, "how about a chorus of 'Auld Lang Syne'?"

"It will make me cry," Grandmother Davies said, "but they will be happy tears, so let's go ahead and sing a verse."

"Should auld acquaintance be forgot..."

Marcie's voice began to break on the words, and she looked up at Peter, trying to blink back the tears.

Tomorrow there would be Ella's famous roast goose dinner, and Mr. Williams had already invited Will Higgins to come over and watch some of the football classics on television with him. Peter and his aunt would be coming, too, so there would be this one last day together.

But, bright and early on the morning of January 2, the Williamses would be starting for Bethesda, and in another few days Marcie would be back at Ashburton High. It seemed to her that she had lived a whole lifetime since her last phone conversation with Brad Evans, when they had been looking for a possible escape route so that she wouldn't have to go to Cape Cod in the middle of winter!

Now Grandmother Davies said, unexpectedly, "Dr. Swan called this afternoon, and he said those X-rays they took yesterday are very encouraging. There's no doubt now that he's going to take this cast off for a Valentine present. I should be able to hobble to Maryland for Easter with all of you — provided I can find a strong young arm to help me along the way!"

She was looking directly at Peter, and as he smiled back at her his eyes never had seemed quite so blue.

"My arm," he said, "has never felt stronger, Mrs. Davies. It is entirely at your disposal, if you'll have it."

"That seems an excellent solution," Mrs. Davies said, nodding wisely. "Of course, I shall have to be going to Maryland again in June, to see Marcie graduate from high school . . ."

Peter's smile broadened. "By June," he said, "I can almost guarantee that my arm will be even stronger!"

It was his turn now to look thoughtful. He said, "I know you have marvelous recovery powers, Mrs. Davies. Dr. Swan told me, when he was taking a look at my cut, that you are one of his most amazing patients. But I would think it still might help to have a young woman around the house this summer. No offense to you, Ella," he added hastily, looking toward the housekeeper.

"You know, Peter," Ella said, her Cape Cod accent very flat, "I've been conjecturing along those same lines myself. I'm not getting any younger. I'd hate to have a stranger about though. Now, if Marcie . . ."

Marcie broke in, "I'm submitting my job application right now," she said.

"Then you're as good as hired," Ella retorted, before Mrs. Davies could even speak.

"Seems to me we're starting out this New Year just the way a New Year should be started," Peter said, and he and Marcie exchanged a look filled with love and caring.